THE FUTURE

IS QUEER

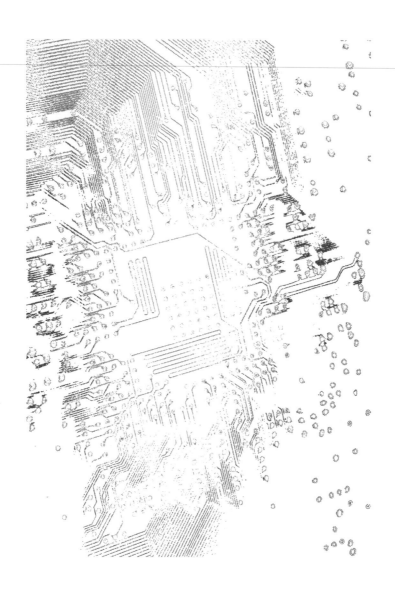

THE FUTURE IS QUEER

edited by RICHARD LABONTÉ
and LAWRENCE SCHIMEL

Arsenal Pulp Press Vancouver

ARSENAL PULP PRESS
200 - 341 Water Street
Vancouver, BC
Canada V6B 1B8
arsenalpulp.com

The publisher gratefully acknowledges the support of the Canada Council
for the Arts and the British Columbia Arts Council for its publishing
program, the Government of Canada through the Book Publishing Industry
Development Program, and the Government of British Columbia through
the Book Publishing Tax Credit Program for its publishing activities.

Text and cover design by Shyla Seller

This is a work of fiction. Any resemblance of characters to persons either
living or deceased is purely coincidental.

"From Homogenous to Honey" © 1988 by Neil Gaiman & Bryan
Talbot, first appeared in *A.A.R.G.H.! (Artists Against Raging Government
Homophobia)*, edited by Alan Moore (self-published, UK: 1988), and is
reprinted with permission.

Printed and bound in Canada

Library and Archives Canada Cataloguing in Publication

   The future is queer : a science fiction anthology / edited by
Richard Labonté and Lawrence Schimel.

ISBN 1-55152-209-8

   1. Gays' writings. 2. Science fiction. 3. Short stories.
4. Fiction – 21st century. 5. Homosexuality – Literary collections.
I. Labonté, Richard, 1949- II. Schimel, Lawrence

PN6120.95.H724F88 2006   823'.0876208353   C2006-903885-6

ISBN13 978-1-55152-209-8

For Asa Dean Liles,
My past, my present, my very queer future
— Richard

In memory of Octavia Butler,
one of our foremost chroniclers of futures
queer and otherwise.
— Lawrence

Contents

INTRODUCTION

My Love Affair with Queer Boys, Gay Lit, and Science Fiction

Richard Labonté

I CAN'T RECALL the first science fiction book I ever read. I know I was reading science fiction by the time I was seven or eight, when I was already bored by the Hardy Boys, the Bobbsey Twins, the Rover Boys, Nancy Drew, Brains Benton, and Tom Swift, whose spacey adventures were my favourite for reading more than once – though I had a thing for those Hardy Boys and their hearty comradeship, too. Perhaps my first time encountering the worlds of "if" was with one of the non-Tarzan books by Edgar Rice Burroughs, when I was eight or nine. Soon I was escaping from the world with *The Chessmen of Mars*, or exploring forgotten worlds in *At the Earth's Core*. I was living then in Paris, a military brat, borrowing English-language books from my father's enlisted male friends (my parents didn't read much beyond the daily newspaper). I recall seeing a large shelf of Burroughs books in our neighbour's living room. I also recall how I liked to wrestle with our neighbour, a single corporal, probably ten years older than me, though he seemed as old as my parents.

When I was ten, my father was transferred to Mont Apica, a now-shuttered Pine Tree Line radar station in the isolated middle of Parc des Laurentides in Quebec: the base was small, 800 or so residents, more than sixty kilometres (thirty-five miles) from the nearest small town, a self-contained village, really: I was able to deliver the daily newspaper bussed in from Montreal to about eighty homes during my school lunch break. There were so few kids my age, boys and girls together, that grades seven, eight, and nine sat in the same classroom, maybe a dozen of us, and families were transferred when their children completed the ninth grade. Add in the kids from the Catholic school across the playground, and we managed to cobble together two softball teams in the summer, and three or four hockey teams in the winter. I was an athletic kid, but not really a team player; I was the catcher in softball, and the goalie in hockey, but ready to head home to a book when the game was over.

There was a small library, tucked away in the basement of the recreation hall, nestled between a two-lane bowling alley and a room where the Boy Scouts met once a week to tie knots. It's a cliché, I know: I learned to do more than tie knots with a few of the boys in my scout patrol. It was an early, untroubled queer sexual initiation. I also set pins in the bowling alley, sometimes handling both lanes myself, more often paired with a French-Canadian boy a year or two older than me, twelve or thirteen; we perched side-by-side while waiting for pins to fall, sweaty in the stuffy air, bumping shoulders and thighs and feeling up each other's biceps. Boy Scouts and bowling: young lust.

But the library was where I fell in love. With Robert Heinlein, Andre Norton, Jack Williamson, A. E. van Vogt, Murray Leinster, E.E. "Doc" Smith, Manly Wade Wellman, and Jack Vance, among many – a universe of imaginations conjuring a wealth of universes. Endless great escape. This was in 1960, and it was the first time, but not the last, that I lost myself in a room full of books. It wasn't a large room: there were perhaps 5,000 volumes, every one donated by families and bachelor officers and young, not-yet-married enlisted men. I remember an awful lot of *Reader's Digest* condensed editions. A lot of mysteries, but they weren't of interest to me then. And a lot of science fiction, enough to keep me reading for a year, until one day a card fell out of a newer book, an invitation to join the Science Fiction Book Club, which I did, in 1961. I was twelve then, and for the next seventeen or so years, until I moved to Los Angeles in 1979 to help open the first branch of A Different Light Bookstore, I ordered every book, every month – except for the Edgar Rice Burroughs titles: his stories were for little kids....

So there I was, a practicing fag by the time I was twelve, and reading four or five science fiction books a week. My future was certainly going to be queer.

My future also became more homosexual, thanks to that same small library at the base. That's where, as I browsed the stacks, I discovered – again, I can't recall My First Literary Time; as I age, I regret I never kept an adolescent diary or an adult journal – a book by Gore Vidal, or Tennessee Williams, or Mary Renault. And just as I found my physical queer self in the raucous, musty bowling alley, back where the lights were dim, I found my literary queer self in that cramped, fusty library with its bright lights. I discovered a daisy chain of writers writing about people like me. Vidal led me to Williams, Williams led me to James Baldwin, Baldwin led me to Truman Capote, Capote led me to Paul Bowles, Bowles led me to William Burroughs, and Mary Renault taught me about both lesbians and lithe Spartan lads: a covert group of queer writers who blurbed each other's books. Ronald Firbank was in there, too, as were John Horne Burns, and Paul Goodman, and Fritz Peters, and Christopher Isherwood.

In all, there were probably fewer than twenty books, maybe thirty, that whispered *gay boy, read me* as I went through that library, shelf by shelf and book by book. And remember: military families and single men who rotated through Mont Apica every two or three years donated them all. Obviously, there were homos among them – John Rechy's *City of Night* popped out of a dusty box in 1963! – though it was certainly possible that a well-read family's personal library included novels by Capote or Baldwin or Renault.

By the time my father was transferred, late in the same year that Rechy steamed up a young boy's glasses (my mother was awfully lenient about the books I brought home, and had in fact given the librarian a letter permitting me to read anything I wanted, though I hid *City of Night* from her prying eyes), I was a practicing homosexual, an avid SF fan (I discovered fanzines around the same time), and unusually well-read, for a young teenager, in the classical homosexual *oeuvre*. I've stayed that way for the forty years since. Well-read, that is, not a teenager. But reading SF keeps me young at heart.

A coda to my pubescent love affair with the genre: Three years after I segued from Arthur C. Clarke to John Rechy, when I was living on the St. Hubert military base outside of Montreal, delivering boxes of groceries and cases of beer on my bicycle to people in the married quarters, I met a man who was transferring out, and he asked if he could hire me to help him box up some old magazines. No hanky-panky ensued, alas: but that's when I acquired more than 1,000 old SF/fantasy pulps: *Amazing* and *Astounding* and *Astonishing*, *Future Fiction* and *Infinity* and *Other Worlds*, *Satellite* and *Startling* and *Spaceway*, *Weird Tales* and *Thrilling Wonder* and *Venture*. There were hundreds of the digests as well, *The Magazine of Fantasy & Science Fiction* and *Galaxy* and those *Worlds of If*. I spent the next several years reading them. In 1980, the collection – expanded by the hundreds of magazines I had bought myself since 1965 – were destroyed when the barn in which they were stored after my move to Los Angeles burned down. To this day, the alluring scent of an old pulp magazine gives me a memory hard-on. And I still pick up an *Analog* or an *Asimov's* or an *F&SF* when I spot them on an unusually well-stocked newsstand....

Which brings me to 2006, and *The Future is Queer*, an anthology synthesizing two of my favourite things: the vivid imaginations of SF writers with a literary bent, and the many permutations of queer worlds to come. There are several worlds imagined in this visionary collection: a future where clones forbidden sex nonetheless explore their emotional and physical needs; a future where too much tolerance is suffocating; a future where bisexual women and men are persecuted more for religious faith than sexual preference; a future where gender choice is magical and mythical; a future where virtual reality offers a lonely woman one more chance to revisit her dead lover; a future – eerily like an hallucinatory present – where a woman's lover returns to haunt her; and – even more darkly – a future where every reference to gay life and art is being scrubbed from existence, and a future where gays in the military have earned the right to be fodder.

Lawrence Schimel and I received more than 100 submissions; I narrowed those down to a couple of dozen, he made the final selection, and the result is an astonishing collection of visionary – and entertaining – stories. This book was his concept; I'm delighted he asked me to help him shape it for you all.

Perth, Ontario, Canada
July 2006

INTRODUCTION

Looking in All Directions

Lawrence Schimel

THE FUTURE HAS long been the purview of science fiction – and that future has increasing implications for queer women and men. The gay marriage controversy, scientific "breakthroughs," and well-organized anti-gay campaigns by the Religious Right seem to ensure that we are still decades away from achieving any kind of pansexual utopia some forty years after the advent of gay liberation.

Nonetheless, despite recent setbacks in some countries, – most prominently, the US – legal recognition of gay and lesbian marriages is taking place and, slowly but inexorably, moving forward. The further one looks to the future, the further technological advances – cloning, gene manipulation, etc. – will erode the biological imperative for heterosexuality as a means of procreation, making the social stigma against same-sex relations even less relevant. Additionally, the continued development of artificial intelligences, as well as improvements in surgery and technology that allow one to redefine and reassign one's gender with greater ease and accuracy, explode our current notions of how we create and modify our identities.

The Future is Queer set out to address these issues, to create a visionary handbook or manual, with stories firmly rooted in the queer present (and past) and extrapolating possible futures.

Science fiction as a literary genre has long provided a welcoming haven for writing and speculation about alternative sexuality. Feminist literature, as well, has a long tradition of utopian fiction. Since we believe the future is not binary, *The Future is Queer* draws from both these literary traditions.

Herein you'll find stories about the legal and social ramifications of cloning, the future of transgender spirituality, gays in the military, the splitting of identities taken to literal extremes, and even nostalgia for the repressive past – but always focused on the *human* angle of these socio-political or technological changes or innovations.

Nearly a decade ago, I co-edited *PoMoSexuals*, an anthology of personal essays that challenged essentialist notions about gender and identity. I like to think of *The Future is Queer* as a fictional sequel or companion to that collection. At first, Richard and I set out with a very strict notion of the type of stories we were looking for: what is generally described as near-future, social science fiction, depicting plausible, possible realities. We weren't looking for bug-eyed aliens or space operas, which belong as much to the genre of fantasy as they do to science fiction.

But just as the journey of writing doesn't always strictly follow the outline one has created before beginning a book, these strictures did get loosened in the end, to include what might be interpreted as future-based fantasy. So while there are no aliens or extra-terrestrial adventures, there are tales that draw on myth and archetype to extrapolate the queer fairy tales or fables of the future.

As with any anthology, it is impossible to please every reader – or even the editors! We argued for (and against) the inclusion of one story or another, and came to reasoned compromises which tried to satisfy as many concerns (personal, the number and citizenship of contributors, our budget, the publishing schedule and other deadlines, the overall shape of the book, etc.) as possible. Our differences of opinion have worked to create what we believe is a stronger anthology, different from what would have resulted if either of us had worked on this project alone.

Submissions arrived from around the globe, through an open call as well as by special solicitation of specific writers whose work we admired; as a result, the book includes a mix of work by first- or second-timers and stories from well-established authors.

The contributors have a wide range of self-proclaimed sexual orientations: heterosexual, gay, lesbian, bisexual, transgender – not that we asked, since it's none of our business. In any event, content was more important for this collection than issues of authorial identity, although we did look particularly for writing that was conscious of current gay, lesbian, bisexual, and transgender identity politics, even if positing a world that moved beyond such concerns. We wanted stories that used the future to talk about issues from our queer past and present, looking in all directions at once.

The resulting mix includes provocative stories, authors, and themes you wouldn't otherwise come across. We hope this book will surprise you and challenge how you think about the world, in one way or another.

THANKS ARE DUE to a number of people who, during the course of our compiling this anthology, helped in one way or another. In particular, I'd like to acknowledge: first and foremost, the many authors who submitted work for this anthology, whether or not we were able to use their stories; Brian Lam and Robert Ballantyne, for having faith in Richard and me and believing in this project; Nalo Hopkinson and Jameson Currier for suggestions; Claude

Lalumière and Kyle Greenwood for extraordinary patience; and finally my co-editor, Richard Labonté, for many years of friendship.

Madrid, Spain
July 2006

Obscure Relations

L. Timmel Duchamp

FROM THE AIR, the deep blue expanse of the ocean looked flat except for the myriad blisters of light pocking the surface. Ezekiel pressed his face against the window; his body fizzed with excitement, as though a promise that had been made to him were about to be kept.

For weeks he had been telling Daniel that he missed the sea, but he had really meant that he missed his home. Now that he had permanent residences in four cities, sycophants to keep him constant company, and virtually the entire world in which to be at home, he had no reason for missing his old world. But the behaviour mods had altered his personality and self-presentation, not his most private, interior *feelings.* "It will be restful there," he had told Daniel. "I'm sick of people. I need a break."

Ezekiel had been letting Daniel call the shots because he knew that to pass successfully as Josiah he needed Daniel to guide and instruct him 24/7. Every time he attended a meeting or a social function, he received instructions from Daniel through his implant. Daniel even provided him with the appropriate responses in casual conversation. He simply wasn't prepared to flatly assert his will, as Josiah would have done.

But although he was clueless about the world, Ezekiel knew a few things about Daniel. Not many days after he had given up trying to persuade Daniel to let him take a break at the compound, Ezekiel said to him, "I just got another email from that woman." Ezekiel had been dodging Lucy Luhmann's calls and ignoring her emails since the day he had replaced Josiah. "She says she's going to visit me here in D.C. next week. Only when I tell her to her face that it's over will she believe it. What the fuck am I going to do? If she gets within ten feet of me she'll know I'm not Josiah." Daniel at once grasped the gravity of the threat. Despite his misgivings about "returning to the scene of the crime," he ordered a tactical retreat. By the end of the week the staff had canceled all of Josiah's pending engagements and disseminated suitable spin on the move.

Until Ezekiel, Daniel, and Josiah's great-nephew Gabriel had murdered him, Josiah had been in the habit of visiting the compound at least once a month. The compound's staff likely assumed that after putting Ezekiel down Josiah had lost all personal interest in the clones. Not that Ezekiel cared what the compound's *staff* thought. But he felt certain that Josiah's appearance on the scene would make the clones anxious, and that bothered him. Short of telling them that he was in fact Ezekiel, that Josiah was the one who was dead, he could do nothing to ease their distress.

As the compound came into view, Ezekiel's pulse quickened. He recalled longing for the freedom to leave it – and his conviction, when he finally had left it, that he would never willingly return. That recollection led to other memories – his bitterness at having been born to a sentence of life imprisonment, his fantasies of the world beyond the compound's walls, his impatience with his fellow clones, who accepted the status quo as though it were as fixed and natural as the rhythms of the tides and the rising and setting of the sun. Thinking back on his life in the compound, it seemed to him now that he had been suspended in a kind of childhood for forty-five years. He no longer entertained those old naïve fantasies, of course; but the bitterness....

The helicopter landed on the concrete bull's eye that he used to think of as a magic portal. As he stepped down onto the pavement, he saw Jerry VanSant, the compound's security officer, and Walter Loman, the doctor in charge of the clones, waiting at the edge of the helipad to greet him. The sight of Loman, slight and dull in his usual khaki shirt and pants that rippled violently in the chopper's backwash, made the back of his neck prickle. After his fellow clones, Loman was the person most likely to make him.

Ezekiel and Daniel shook hands with Loman and VanSant as the chopper lifted. The racket of the rotors and engine roared in Ezekiel's ears even after the craft had swung around and begun retracing its route back to the airfield. Watching the chopper recede, Ezekiel broke into a cold sweat. *Daniel's right. This is insane!*

"JOSIAH?"

Ezekiel became aware of Daniel's hand on his shoulder and pulled himself together. Without a word to anyone, he started briskly for the house. Loman and VanSant, trotting after him, quickly covered over his brusqueness with a lot of deferential chatter about how happy they were that the weather had cleared. They'd had a bad storm earlier in the week; it had changed the shape of the beach, as he'd see – had swept in a hell of a lot of driftwood down near the mouth of the estuary. Loman said something about putting the clones to work clearing it away, that the beach was useless now for jogging since there was no clear path.

VanSant held open the side door into the house. "This is a working vacation," Ezekiel said to Loman. He walked past VanSant, who looked exactly as he had the day Ezekiel had left – stocky and bulked up, his thick, black hair gleaming with grease, his black denim uniform reeking of cigarette smoke. But though VanSant struck Ezekiel as exactly the same, the place itself seemed strange. The house looked small, felt small. As though the scale wasn't right. As though he'd grown, or his old home had shrunk. His sense of disorientation faintly nauseated him.

Ezekiel glanced at VanSant and Loman. "Got a few things to attend to this afternoon. But I'll see *you*, Walter" – Ezekiel made a gun of his finger and pointed it at Loman, exactly as Josiah had often done – "at dinner."

As he climbed the stairs to Josiah's suite, Ezekiel realized for the first time that although Walter Loman was a free man with a legal existence, he led nearly as confined a life as the clones did. Presumably he told himself that this confinement was worth it. And yet, now that Ezekiel had been out in the world, ambitions that had previously seemed overweening to him looked puny, and the doctor's research project on the order of bean counting. What kind of emotional life could the man have? VanSant, at least, had drinking buddies and a sex life. Daniel had friends and a significant other. But Loman....

Loman is one sick puppy, man.

In a way, Loman was more bent than even Josiah had been. Ezekiel could almost understand Josiah having developed a fascination with the clones once he'd begun having them made. Although they served as living repositories of customized parts, available on demand, they were also doppelgangers of himself, soulless, personality-modified, and living in an artificial state of nature – a biologically material version of virtual beings. Ezekiel suspected that a less self-assured man than Josiah would have found them more creepy than fascinating. But if he, Josiah's favourite clone, had ever given Josiah the creeps, he had never seen any hint of it.

"I'll be up in a few minutes," Daniel said when they reached the fourth level.

"What's the rush?" Ezekiel said. "I thought we were on vacation." He continued alone up the stairs, then hesitated when he reached the top. The fifth level, Josiah's private space, had always been forbidden territory. It was also the site of Josiah's murder; he supposed that was why it felt weirdly taboo. He'd never really had the chance to take full psychological possession of it after Josiah's death.

The thick, dark red carpet muffled his footsteps as he wandered through the suite to familiarize himself with the layout. The windows faced west, of course, as well as north and south. He opened the French doors to the deck off the sitting room, and the surf whispered in his ears. It was a sound that had been in his blood from birth, a sound he had been missing for months now. He stepped out onto the deck and closed his eyes; drawing in the fresh sea air, pulling it deep into his lungs, he let the rhythm of the surf pound through his body.

He was home.

When he heard a shout and some laughter, he opened his eyes. He made a quick scan of the beach and found Jonathan, Ezra, and Micah just below the deck, tossing a Frisbee. Jonathan looked happy and carefree, leaping with the lank energy he could not, at eighteen, repress. Ezra's shoulders, though, were hunched, and by the way he held his head Ezekiel guessed he was snatching glances at the decks and windows, looking for signs of Josiah's presence. Though Micah's posture wasn't defensive, every time the Frisbee came to him he threw it with such force that it sailed high over Jonathan and Ezra's heads, sending them chasing after it. Ezekiel had never looked at them in quite this way before, never been so conscious of how physically distinct they were. He noted that the hard, lean lines of Jonathan's body flowed with easy grace, in marked contrast to the solid, powerful muscle of Ezra's. And he saw that although Micah was only two years older than Jonathan, there was already a heaviness in his jaw, a thickening in his neck.

"Josiah?"

Ezekiel said, without turning, "What is it, Daniel?" He heard the familiar Josiah-rasp in his own voice and reflexively flinched – only to recall that that voice was now *his*. Daniel always assumed that he was at his beck and call. Would that ever change? Ezekiel pressed himself against the railing in order to conceal his erection. His knuckles, as he gripped the ledge, went white.

Daniel came out onto the deck. "I just got messaged by Jorgesson's aide. She wants to conference with you as soon as possible."

Ezekiel smiled. "Which happens to be Tuesday afternoon." He was not about to work over the weekend.

"No, Josiah. It's got to be *now*."

Daniel's voice was so loud and peremptory that Ezekiel wasn't surprised to see Micah and Jonathan both look up. When they saw that he was staring at them, they quickly ducked their heads and moved out of view. Feeling thwarted, Ezekiel turned his head and gave Daniel a look that was pure Josiah.

Daniel's eyes narrowed. Frowning, he crossed his arms over his chest. "She's organizing an override of the president's veto of the Sanctity of the Human Soul bill and wants to be sure you're on board. If you tell her she can be sure of your vote and that you'll help marshal support from the wafflers, it won't take more than a few minutes."

"But I'm not going to vote to override," Ezekiel said. "So just message her aide back and let her know I won't be available until Tuesday."

"Not going to vote to override! Have you lost your *mind*?"

Despite his effort to suppress it, a smile broke over Ezekiel's face. Since he had no wish to antagonize Daniel, he turned his head and pointed at the bald eagle circling above the rocks perhaps twenty-five yards south of the compound. "Haven't seen an eagle since I've been away," he said.

"Don't change the subject."

Ezekiel looked at Daniel. "No, I haven't lost my mind – I've developed it. What kind of sense would it make for *me* to support that bill?"

Daniel bent over the railing and scanned the area. "They've gone in," he said, then lowered his voice – "but it's still not safe. Step inside, Josiah." He shot Ezekiel a fierce look and held out his arm, gesturing Ezekiel off the deck.

They went in, and Daniel closed the French doors and faced Ezekiel. "That damned bill has Josiah's name on it," he said. "Which is to say, *your* name. That bill is Josiah Taylor's baby. And now Josiah Taylor is not only *not* going to help his colleagues organize a defence of it, he's actually going to vote against it? What kind of sense will *that* make to the world?"

"Relax, Daniel." Ezekiel's voice mellowed. "Josiah Taylor has had a change of heart. He's done a lot of soul-searching and has seen that he made a mistake that he'd be glad to have the president undo. It's that simple."

"Simple." Daniel put his hands to his head. "Jesus." He rubbed his face. "Now look, my friend. Though you've been in office less than a year, you've made your name with this bill. It's about all anyone in politics knows about you." Daniel always explained his imperatives. "But trust me, if you disavow it at this stage, that's *all* you'll ever be known for. And you'll be pissing off a huge number of lobbyists who'll likely target your seat five years from now." He pinched the bridge of his nose and pressed his index finger midway between his eyebrows, prompting Ezekiel to wonder whether he had a sinus headache. "I don't get it, Zeke. This bill was your doing. Not your ... predecessor's."

"Josiah cooked it up with Jorgesson before he even took office," Ezekiel said. "Josiah's staffers were already writing the language when I arrived in D.C., and you took charge of it. I didn't know what the hell I was doing – or who the hell I was. I just wanted to keep people from suspecting I might not be Josiah."

"And you don't think you have to do that now?" As a co-conspirator, Daniel, like Gabriel, had as much to lose from discovery as Ezekiel did.

Ezekiel answered with a shrug and fetched himself a bottle of juice from the fridge built into the breakfront.

Daniel said, "In case you haven't realized it yet, politicians often take positions that are in conflict with their private views."

Ezekiel sat on the sofa and propped his legs on the coffee table. "You bought all that stuff Josiah was always spouting about our being *copies*, didn't you." Ezekiel himself had bought it.

"What I think is irrelevant," Daniel said. "What matters is your political career."

Ezekiel practically inhaled the grapefruit juice. He loved the smell, adored the feel of it prickling on his tongue. That he'd had to wait forty-five years for his first taste of it made every encounter a heady experience; its sharpness invigorated him and piqued his appetite. He looked at Daniel and smiled. "It took me a while to pick up on this, but what I think is that because you took me for a weak copy, you assumed you'd be able to manipulate me like a puppet. Or icon. It didn't occur to you that I might find Josiah's life utterly tedious. And that I might start *wanting*. As real people do. Isn't that, after all, what an independent consciousness does? *Want*? And then act on that *want*?"

Daniel looked stunned.

So it's true, Ezekiel thought. It *didn't* occur to him.

Moving slowly, Daniel sank heavily onto the sofa opposite. "Tell me, then. If you don't want political power, Josiah, what do you want?"

Ezekiel couldn't tell if Daniel had called him "Josiah" on purpose or not, and so he didn't understand the significance of the usage. He swallowed more juice before replying, but got no closer to understanding. "I'm not sure," he said. "Except that I want some kind of real life. About which I still actually know zilch. I'm tired of feeling like I'm playing a role."

Daniel snorted. "Don't be an idiot." His voice grew harsh. "When you assume another person's identity, playing a role is the first requirement of survival."

"That's not what I'm talking about," Ezekiel said. "What I want is to make my own life – strike off on my own path. Not live Josiah's fucking boring future in his place."

Daniel looked uneasy. "What exactly did you have in mind?"

Ezekiel paused a moment to savour the thought of Daniel's inevitable reaction. Then he said: "Inform Loman that I want Jonathan to join us for dinner." For Jonathan was what he wanted. He'd been wanting him for months, though he hadn't realized it until he'd opened the bottle of juice and the sharp, fruity aroma of the grapefruit had tickled his nose.

Given who he now was, Ezekiel saw no reason he couldn't have Jonathan.

It HAD BEEN Josiah's custom to make an inspection of the compound shortly following arrival. Daniel advised Ezekiel to forego it, but Ezekiel thought that breaking with the habit of decades would draw Loman's attention – and perhaps his scrutiny. So at around three-thirty that afternoon, Ezekiel went down to the ground floor to begin the tour.

Loman, he knew, would have had the clones scrubbing and polishing for several days before Josiah's arrival; he had probably put them through a major inspection before breakfast that morning. As he padded down the last half-flight of steps, he glimpsed one of the youngsters streaking past, headed in the direction of the pool. By the time he reached the bottom of the stairs he could hear the boy warning, "Number One's on his way down!"

Ezekiel didn't go directly to the pool or gym but began with the dining room. The room was immaculate, even the linoleum floor, which no matter how often it was swept seemed always in Ezekiel's memory to have been gritty with crumbs (except, of course, during Josiah's visits). The long wall opposite the windows was still covered with the chart of chore assignments, and the short wall with dozens of plaques, each one documenting the annual award Josiah made to the "fittest" clone. Ezekiel remembered every one of the prizes bestowed on him those few times when he had been pronounced the fittest – a watch, a surf board, a pair of flippers and a snorkel, mirrored shades, a personal radio, a dragon kite made of silk. He didn't know why, but the memories brought him close to tears.

"I think everything's in order, sir," Loman said from the doorway.

Ezekiel turned. "So, Walter. Let's take a gander at the boys' sleeping quarters, shall we?" Ezekiel spent a minute or so per room. Each was as he remembered – save his own. He alone had been allotted a private room as the privilege of the eldest, and that privilege, apparently, had not been passed down to Judah, the next in seniority, for the room had been fitted with racks and hooks for holding sweat suits, underwear, shoes, and socks, as well as the clones' entire collection of surf boards.

All the bunk beds in the dorms were made with square-cornered military precision. The urinals and basins in the washroom gleamed, as though they had been installed only that morning. And the rec room, ordinarily a chaotic mess of chairs and cushions strewn with water bottles, sweat bands, and dirty socks, looked unnaturally neat – and dreary. Of all the rooms in the clones' quarters, the rec room held the bitterest of memories. Night after night he had watched the vid screen with the others, treated to reality shows, which most of the guys favoured over sportscasts – taking them for portraits of the world outside, a world they would never be allowed even to visit.

Ezekiel took a quick look at the gym to confirm that the equipment was properly maintained, then went on to the pool, hot and bright with the sun beating down through the ceiling of skylights. The clones waited, standing in line ordered by age, and with the exception of little Eli, who had been the look-out and so was wearing shorts and a T-shirt, all of them were just out of the pool, dripping and naked. Beginning with Judah, Ezekiel moved down the line, pausing before each clone in turn, looking him over and making Josiah-comments. Judah was five years younger than Ezekiel, but now that Ezekiel had begun getting all the treatments and drugs Josiah had habitually received, Judah looked older than Ezekiel. As Josiah always did, Ezekiel asked Jeptha how "the arm" was "coming along." And he praised Ezra for the marked improvement he had shown in his latest cardio-vascular stress test. Ezekiel knew for a fact that all of them were flattered that Josiah called them by name and kept track of what they'd been up to, and that they saved their resentment for Loman, who drove them. Only he had detested Josiah, only Ezekiel had understood that Loman's regime suited Josiah perfectly.

Ezekiel cut short his inspection and told Loman he would be dropping in from time to time over the course of the week. Leaving the house, he felt as though he were escaping it. The air was fresh and clean, the water radiant. He enjoyed climbing the steep, scrubby slope and walking the perimeter, following the electrified fence the length of the property as Josiah had always done. Walking the perimeter felt different, now that he possessed the freedom to leave whenever he chose. Still, echoes of his old frustration eventually reached him, and his pleasure dulled. For a few minutes he even wondered why he had risked discovery by returning to the scene of the crime.

But then he went down to the beach, and his spirits lifted. He spent a couple of hours alone, walking along the waterline, climbing over and around the trash left by the storm, and his consciousness of being an imposter melted away, as though by magic. Free of the clamour of voices that ordinarily surrounded him, ceaselessly imposing their idea of who Josiah was and must be, constantly demanding Josiah-responses of him, he could actually hear himself think. Breathing in the moist salt air, savoring the ruffle of the wind through his hair, he eked out an insight that until now had been blocked: he needed to make the identity of Josiah his own, not simply a mask he donned for most of his waking hours. That, he thought, was what he had been trying to tell Daniel without realizing it, for breaking with the established habits, deeds, and attitudes of Josiah Taylor was the most obvious way to accomplish the integration. He needed first, though, to make Daniel understand that he couldn't spend the rest of his life in masquerade, that that way lay madness.

EZEKIEL WENT TO dinner more relaxed than he'd been in months. He took it for a sign when standing at Josiah's place at the table, rubbing his hands together as Josiah used to do, sweeping his gaze over his minions and shooting a grin at Jonathan, that it felt right and natural. Daniel had explained that Josiah had given up cocktails in the den before dinner, and so Loman, Daniel, and Jonathan had all been standing near their chairs, waiting for his arrival. Daniel had also warned the cook that Josiah no longer ate meat, which Ezekiel's digestion could not handle. "You're looking good!" he said to Jonathan, and to Loman, "Lot of work to be done, cleaning up the beach. It's like a junkyard out there. But good exercise for the boys, eh, Walter?" He had sat at Josiah's table so many times over the decades that Josiah's every habitual gesture and speech mannerism came naturally. And yet because Jonathan in no way resembled Ezekiel, Ezekiel's interactions with him in no way resembled Josiah's interactions with himself.

Jonathan had every reason to resent and fear Josiah for having "put down" Ezekiel, but Ezekiel detected not the slightest trace of suppressed anger. Jonathan even laughed several times during the soup course when Ezekiel recounted stories about "those folks in D.C." Ezekiel sensed that Daniel disliked the friendly tone of his badinage with Jonathan, but he also perceived that Loman saw nothing odd in it. Loman, after all, had never viewed the clones as identical, indistinguishable personalities: even if their ages hadn't made each of them easily identifiable, their personalities and mannerisms would have sufficed to do so.

As the soup course was cleared, Ezekiel gazed past Loman, through the wall of windows, at the sun, sinking below the horizon in a blaze of orange and dark indigo painting the surface of the water. Conventional wisdom produces clichés for every conceivable situation. Whether one prated *like to like* or *opposites attract*, neither – or both – applied here. Jonathan's DNA was virtually identical to his own because they had both been cloned from Josiah's. And yet Jonathan was so entirely different from himself. Ezekiel had helped raise him – could remember the day Loman brought Jonathan's infant self into the compound and apportioned out the childcare among them, adding caring for Micah, who had been only two years old at the time, to their duties. In marked contrast to Ezekiel's brusque and touchy disposition, Jonathan had always been affectionate and easy; Jonathan got his way through charm, Ezekiel through bullying. But likely the biggest difference between them lay in Ezekiel's penchant for risk-taking. Jonathan *always* played it safe.

So when Ezekiel asked Loman for a report on the boys' performances in the gym that day and then teased Jonathan for having let Ezra, twelve years his senior, out-swim him, and Saul, seventeen years his senior, out-lift him, Jonathan laughed. "I guess I'm not all that competitive, sir," he said. "Except that I'll do what I have to not to come in last." His eyes sparkled in the light of the chandelier, which seemed to grow brighter as dark rolled over the ocean and the windows turned into black mirrors, offering an image of another dining room behind Loman.

Ezekiel knew as well as Jonathan that Jeptha, handicapped with a slowly regenerating arm temporarily supplemented with a prosthesis until all the tissue had finished growing, nearly always came in last. And he also knew, though Loman did not, that the clones felt the urge to compete only when they weren't being monitored. "Not competitive?" Ezekiel said in Josiah's grand manner. "How can that be?" He snorted. "I suppose there's no point, then, in teaching you to play chess."

Jonathan's gaze dropped to his plate, and a dull flush crept from his neck to scalp. Ezekiel avoided Daniel's eye and ate the last bite of eggplant on his plate. Taking care to make his tone indifferent, he ordered the salad course served.

Loman said, "I've observed that none of the other copies are as competitive as Ezekiel was."

Copies: a word that would never cross Josiah's lips again.

Loman speared a chunk of tomato, thrust it into his mouth, and quickly swallowed. He shot Ezekiel a look of triumph. "You see, sir, my hypothesis is that being the oldest made a significant difference."

A stark silence settled over the table as Daniel and Ezekiel picked at their plates of mixed greens and Jonathan sat with his eyes downcast and his hands in his lap. Loman, shoving his salad into his mouth at speed, kept looking from Ezekiel to Daniel, as though he expected encouragement to expand on his theory. To keep him from doing so, Ezekiel said to Jonathan, "You know how to play gin, boy?"

Jonathan looked at him, and Ezekiel saw the bleakness naked in his eyes. Some sort of thrill shivered through him, a sensation he did not recognize and was not sure how to interpret.

"Yes, sir. We play it downstairs a lot."

"Good." Ezekiel's voice had gotten husky. "Then you can give me a game now." He pushed back his chair and got to his feet.

"Josiah," Daniel said. *His* voice was sharp. "There's that matter we talked about earlier —"

"I've given you my decision, Daniel."

"Ten minutes is all I ask," Daniel said. And now his tone said, *Don't push me, Zeke, or you'll be sorry.*

Ezekiel sighed. "Very well. Ten minutes. In my sitting room." He looked at Jonathan, who was standing beside his chair, waiting for an order. "And I'll see *you*, boy, in the den in fifteen."

TWENTY-FIVE MINUTES later, Ezekiel walked into the den. He saw at a glance that the leather chairs and sofas grouped around the redwood-slab coffee table were unoccupied. He did not see Jonathan. The only illumination came from the lamp behind Josiah's chair, so most of the room was in shadow. As Ezekiel moved toward the desk in the corner to use the house phone, he found Jonathan stretched out on the rug behind one of the sofas, lying on his stomach, his eyes closed and his lips parted. His shirt had ridden up, exposing a strip of skin just above the waistband of his shorts; his shoulders rose and fell with each regular breath. Ezekiel stared at him as though he'd never seen him before. As though they hadn't taken hundreds of saunas together. As though he hadn't changed Jonathan's damned diapers when he was a baby.

Ezekiel turned and closed the door. He leaned back against it and listened to the surf, which was muted because the room faced east, listened to Jonathan's breathing, which was light and steady and faster in sleep than Ezekiel's when awake. These were the sounds of his life history: the endless thud of the surf, the continual inhaling and exhaling of his fellow clones; they were as intimate as the rhythm of the movement of his own blood. He thought about what he wanted and what he could do, and he crossed the room on tiptoe. Standing near Jonathan's feet, he studied him closely, taking in his bony ankles and well-muscled calves, his powerful thighs spread wide and barely covered by his shorts, his strong neck and broad shoulders, and flashed on the last time they'd been in the sauna together, when it had been just the two of them and Ezekiel's cock had gotten hard for the second time in his adult life, the day after the mod blocking him from sexual arousal had been removed. The image of Jonathan lying on his back on the bench opposite, unaware of Ezekiel's arousal, had burned itself into his memory. It filled his mind every time he had an erection. And though Jonathan's body here and now filled his gaze, the excitement of that moment in the sauna overlaid all his perceptions.

He was hard now. Throbbing. Stiffer than he could remember. He inched forward and dropped to his knees. He reached out to touch that beckoning strip of exposed skin. His hunger was so immense that his entire body was shaking.

For all of his adult life the only thing he had ever really wanted was to escape his confinement in the compound and be treated as though he were a real person, with a soul. And with Daniel's help, he *had* escaped. And so he had become a real person with real choices — choices, he discovered, that he couldn't care very much about because all of them flowed from the life-script someone else had written. But now he wanted *this*. He wanted Jonathan. This was his, Ezekiel's choice, not Josiah's.

That he wanted Jonathan told him something about who, besides Josiah's impersonator, he was and who he might, in the future, become.

The heat of Jonathan's body touched his fingers even before his fingers touched Jonathan's skin. He glanced at Jonathan's face to see if the touch had woken him and laid his palm flat against the skin. The sensation of the touch ran through him like an electrical charge. Both wanting him to awaken and wanting him to continue sleeping, Ezekiel slipped his fingers under the waistband of Jonathan's shorts. As his hand felt the shape of Jonathan's cheeks and discovered the crack between them, his heart beat so fast and so hard that he imagined it exploding out of his chest.

Jonathan stirred. "Hey," he said, turning on his side and half-sitting up. He squinted at Ezekiel, as though to see which of them was playing some dumb trick on him. His brows drew in. "Zeke –" His mouth dropped open, then closed to let his teeth gnaw his lower lip.

Ezekiel withdrew his hand and sat back on his heels. When he had his breath under control, he said in his amused-Josiah voice, "You know better than that, boy." His heart was still racing, though, and his body trembling, but not, he realized, with fear. The changes flitting over Jonathan's face reminded him that while he might not be in full command of himself, he did have command of the situation – and Jonathan.

Jonathan rubbed the sleep from his eyes with his right middle finger. He said, "Yeah. Sorry. I was half-asleep."

Ezekiel said, "Take off your shorts."

Jonathan stared at Ezekiel. After a few seconds, his cheeks blazed blood-red. "Is that why he tried to kill you?" He looked stricken with confusion. "I mean, did you want that from Zeke, that night you put him down?"

Ezekiel was thunderstruck. When he could speak again, he

said, "Where on earth did you get the idea that Zeke tried to kill me?"

Jonathan was gnawing his lower lip again. Slowly he sat up; he started to move, to put some distance between them, but Ezekiel laid his hand on his knee to still him. Jonathan said, his voice breathless and unsteady, "He was like a crazy man that last day. Like something in him had snapped. Of course, he always had a kind of aggressive streak." Jonathan laughed uncomfortably. "From about the time I turned twelve he was always shoving me around, saying that *someone* had to knock some sense into me." He laughed again. "For my own good – and also for the rest of us. He was always afraid I'd do something idiotic. And Loman always uses collective punishment, so…." He shrugged and looked away, as though he couldn't handle meeting Ezekiel's gaze. "Anyway. We were all worried, that day, us clones, that he'd snap. At any kind of provocation. That maybe he'd end up killing somebody – you, probably. Or Loman, maybe. So when we heard you'd put him down … well. We just assumed." Jonathan's Adam's apple jerked convulsively. He looked at Ezekiel. "You know." He looked down at his hands. "That he'd tried to kill you."

Jonathan's perspective so overturned everything that Ezekiel had been assuming about the clones and Josiah's death that Ezekiel could not speak.

Jonathan rubbed the back of his neck, and the movement of his arm released a strong whiff of Jonathan-sweat. "I mean, he was your favourite. You wouldn't have killed him on a whim." He looked at Ezekiel, his eyes clear and trusting. "Would you?"

Jesus. He trusts Josiah – over me. Even though Josiah would have helped himself to Micah's heart and lungs if I hadn't killed the old bastard first. And what was that, but a whim? Fairly bristling with anger, Ezekiel was hot to defend himself – and to expose just how little value Josiah had placed on their lives – but he knew that doing so would be suicidal. His body went rigid with the effort to leash his anger. "No," he said gently. "I wouldn't have. Difficult though he could be, I had considerable affection for him. But he really left me no choice." Jonathan nodded, and Ezekiel said, "Enough said on the subject. Clear?"

Jonathan nodded again.

Silence blossomed between them, grew like a thicket. Ezekiel stared at him. When Jonathan cleared his throat, a smile spread over Ezekiel's face. Jonathan scratched his jaw. Finally he said, "So. If we're going to play some gin, maybe you could, um, tell me where to find a deck of cards?"

Ezekiel squeezed Jonathan's knee. "We'll play cards some other time." His hand slid up Jonathan's thigh.

Jonathan's head tilted to the side, and he looked shyly at Ezekiel. "So you want to do … what?"

"What do you think?" Ezekiel tried to imagine what Jonathan thought was going on between them and realized that he could not imagine the same situation ever having arisen between himself and Josiah.

Jonathan laughed nervously. "I'd better not say, or I'll get in trouble. I mean, I've already said more than I should have." He laughed again. "Everyone's always said I talk too much."

"You won't get in trouble with *me*."

Jonathan slid him a sly look and laughed again. "Well, if it weren't you, but one of us clones, I'd have thought you were wanting to fool around."

Ezekiel's smile froze on his face. "Fool around?" Unable to help himself, he looked at Jonathan's crotch. Was it possible that the mod inhibiting the clones' sexuality had for some reason stopped working?

Jonathan's flush recurred. "I'm sure it's not as good as regular sex. 'Cause we can't have orgasms. But we still got nerves, you know, down there. And there're other ways of getting hard."

Ezekiel couldn't believe what he was hearing. "You're saying you all 'fool around' together like that?" He pictured the lot of them screwing together, sharing a secret existence from which they'd pissily excluded him.

"Nah, not *all* of them. Just me and two others." He lifted his chin in defiance. "But don't ask me who they are. 'Cause I don't want to get nobody else in trouble for it."

It was hard to believe. The kid had never been outside the compound his whole life. Couldn't have an erection, much less an orgasm. And yet somehow he had managed to become way more experienced than Ezekiel, whose own sexual experience amounted to half a dozen wet dreams and nine months of masturbating once or twice a day. He said, keeping his voice casual, "You can keep names out of it. But I'm curious to know. How did you even get the idea of doing it, in the first place?"

Jonathan's eyes widened, and Ezekiel wondered at his surprise. "Well, it's not like it started from an *idea*. I mean, it just sort of *happened*. One night in the rec room, when we were all sitting around watching one of those hokey wrestling shows, a couple of the guys got into a wrestling thing of their own. Not like the matches Loman sets up for us, but just messing around. And pretty soon it escalated. And Judah – 'cause Zeke was in his room – yelled at them to either stop it or take it outside. So they did! I mean, they literally went out onto the beach. And when they didn't come in by the next commercial, I got curious and went outside to see what was going on. And what'd happened, see, was that one of them had tugged the other's shorts down to his ankles, and that guy was trying to do the same to the other guy, and, well, by the time I got there, they were stroking each other's balls. They didn't know I was there. Well, I was just a little kid still, and I was always sneaking around … and I sort of crept up behind them and took *my* shorts off, too, 'cause I wanted to know what they were *doing*. And that's how it all started, I guess. And the other guys, they made me swear I wouldn't tell."

And probably, Ezekiel thought, threatened him with dire retaliation if he did. He got to his feet. Staring down at Jonathan, he said, "All it'd take would be one injection to get that mod removed."

Jonathan's eyes brightened, then narrowed. He looked incredulous. "You've never made deals with any of *us* before."

Are you out of your mind, man? The other clones would know. And Loman would go nuts. The whole idea is insane. Step by step, he was working himself deeper and deeper into the shit. What was the matter with him? Why couldn't he control himself? Jonathan was playing him! Ezekiel said, "With you only. I'll make a deal with you."

"I'm listening." Jonathan sounded cautious.

"You fool around with me, and I'll get the mod removed. And then we'll be men together." As if, Ezekiel thought, he had even the faintest idea what that would be.

He held his hand down to Jonathan.

Ezekiel sent Jonathan away before six the next morning in the hope that the boy would be able to slip back into the clones' quarters unobserved. But he had to practically push Jonathan, for when Ezekiel opened the door to let him out, Jonathan grabbed Ezekiel by the shoulders and said, "Hey, you aren't going back on the deal, are you?"

Ezekiel gave him a haughty stare, then seized his wrists and broke his grip. He closed the door. "You doubt my word?"

Jonathan gnawed his lip as he took several seconds to answer what Ezekiel had assumed was a rhetorical question. "If everyone's going to know eventually, why make such a big deal about my sneaking back to my room?"

Worried about the time, just wanting to get Jonathan out of there, Ezekiel swore he had every intention of getting the injection lined up as soon as possible – but added that if Jonathan couldn't play by his rules, the deal would be off. So Jonathan left quietly. He had been fascinated by Ezekiel's orgasms and had decided that he had to have them, too. He knew that Josiah was his only shot at getting them.

Ezekiel paced up and down the length of the sitting room. He tried to picture first Daniel's and then Loman's reaction to his decision. And he thought about how Jonathan had tried to talk him into injections for the two he "fooled around with." It occurred to him that removing the inhibiting mod of only one of them would likely create serious problems among the clones. But favouring the three who were sexually active would make even *more* of a mess....

"What the *fuck* did you think you were doing?"

Ezekiel wheeled to face Daniel. He hadn't heard him come in; Daniel must have used his security access to enter Josiah's quarters.

Daniel railed at him: "What you've done is so wrong, for so many reasons, I can't even begin —" He glared at Ezekiel. "For god's sake, will you put on a robe or something?"

Ezekiel looked down at himself and saw that he was naked. "Oh. Right." He went into the bedroom and opened one mirrored door after another. Finally, at the far left end of the closet, he found at least half a dozen robes rubbing shoulders.

Daniel followed him into the bedroom. "If you thought no one would notice, think again. Loman sure as hell knows. And probably VanSant. And maybe even all the other clones besides."

Some of the robes were cotton, some silk, and at least one was rayon. Ezekiel stared stupidly at them, trying to choose.

"Are you listening to me, man?"

Ezekiel grabbed and wrapped himself in the first robe that came to hand, heavy cotton in a rich burgundy design. "Yes, Daniel, I'm listening."

Daniel was already dressed, in jeans and white shirt. "But

that's not the worst thing about it, the thing that kept me awake most of the night, the thing that made me consider actually risking everything to stop it." He spoke through his teeth. "You don't know, Zeke, just how close I came to charging up here and stopping you."

Ezekiel got the belt of the robe knotted around his waist, then folded his arms over his chest and looked at Daniel – really looked at him. He saw that his adviser's face was too pale, his lips tremulous. "*Stopping* us? *Why?* Because we're clones? Or because having a clone up to share his bed was out of Josiah's character?"

Daniel's eyes flashed. "You fucking sociopath! Is it possible you don't even understand what you've done? What kind of consent can someone who not only is not sexual but is also someone over whom you exercise life-and-death power actually have? I had no idea you were so desperate for a sexual partner – or even that you were gay, for god's sake. If you'd just asked, Jerry and I would've taken you out and shown you where to go to find partners. Since I assumed you were like Josiah, I didn't even consider suggesting it. But to go hitting on someone who isn't even sexual! Jesus! It's fucking tantamount to rape." His hands clenched into fists, and for a few seconds Ezekiel thought he was going to take a swing at him. "But why should I be surprised? You have, after all, about as much moral sense as an animal."

Ezekiel shoved his fists into his pockets, because now *he* was feeling like taking a swing. His mouth twisted into a sneer that was more Ezekiel than Josiah. "Not sexual? Jonathan?" Ezekiel laughed, as though nothing could be more derisory. "That shows how much *you* know!"

Daniel flung a scornful look at him. "Asshole! You think I'm stupid enough to buy that? I know as well as you do that they've all got the same mods you had – and you're not going to try to tell me now that the mods didn't make you about as sexual as a board."

"*I* wasn't sexual. But Jonathan isn't like me. He tells me that in spite of the mod, at least three of them enjoy themselves – *fooling around*, as they call it." Ezekiel grinned at the expression on Daniel's face – a revealing mixture of confusion and outrage. "So you see, last night I asked Jonathan to '*fool around*' with *me*." Ezekiel could see that Daniel wasn't sure he believed him. "And he was happy to."

Daniel shook his head. "I don't get it. What, how –?"

Ezekiel produced a Josiah-chuckle. "So you're curious! Would you like me to tell you what we did last night?"

"No!' Daniel visibly shuddered. "No. Whatever it was, it's bound to be … perverse. And childish." His lips curled with distaste. "And on top of that, it's incest!"

"Really? How do you figure that? You know the text of the Sanctity of the Soul bill better than I do: you helped write it. Clones may share the same DNA, but they're neither brothers nor father and sons – except in cases where the original progenitors legally adopt the clones they've had made. Which Josiah did not do. And it's not like we were brought up to feel kinship on account of our DNA, is it? Since if we were, Josiah would have had to be considered our relative, too. And no one thinks that." Even without the Sanctity of the Soul bill, legally speaking, identical DNA was not a sufficient condition for establishing kinship.

Daniel stalked to the sitting room door. He stopped and turned. "Have you given any thought to what you're going to say to Loman?" His voice was harsh.

Ezekiel's mirth dropped away. "Yes, as a matter of fact, I have. I made a deal with Jonathan that I'd have the mod blocking his sexuality removed, and the more I think about it, the smarter it seems to do it for all of them instead of just my favourite. And so yes, I've been thinking about how I'm going to break the news to Loman."

Daniel's eyes almost bugged out of his head. "For god's sake, Zeke! You can't *do* that! There's a *reason* they've been given that mod. Christ! You're playing with fire!" He shook his head. "But of course it will never come to that. Loman will never accept it." The thought seemed to reassure him – until some new idea occurred to him, one that made him stare accusingly at Ezekiel. "You've got to get hold of yourself, man. It's almost like you *want* us to get caught."

"Don't be ridiculous," Ezekiel said. "But you know, you're wrong about Loman. Because he's not indispensable."

"You're hopeless. You really don't get it, do you?" Daniel shook his head, as if to say that he didn't know how to talk to Ezekiel anymore.

Ezekiel said, "How soon can we get the injections for removing the mod? I'd as soon not go through Gabriel if I don't have to." Ezekiel had enough evidence incriminating Josiah's great-nephew to keep him from making trouble, but he'd be happy never to have to deal with the man again.

Daniel folded his arms over his chest. "You seem to think you can manage Loman. So get him to do it."

"Why not? Do you really think he'd try to cross Josiah?"

Daniel scrubbed his face with his hands.

"Sorry you traded Josiah for me?" Ezekiel said softly.

Daniel's hands fell away from his face. From across the room his gaze locked with Ezekiel's. "Before you do anything, Zeke, you'd damned well better think in terms of what you can survive coming to light. And I'm telling you, you couldn't survive the fallout if it got out that you'd made all the clones sexual. First, there's the hypocrisy factor, because of the Sanctity of the Soul bill. And then there's the fact that your lifting their mods will have the appearance of promoting promiscuity – a promiscuity that'll have the taint of incest on it, regardless of whether or not clones fall outside the definition of family."

Ezekiel leaned back against one of the mirrored closet doors. "It won't come out. Everyone who works here has signed a non-disclosure agreement. And Loman knows that if he blows his, he'll *never* get professional recognition for his longitudinal study, since no reputable journal would publish without my permission. And all he's ever cared about is his precious unique data collected in the closest thing to laboratory conditions possible with humans."

Daniel was silent for a moment. And then he said, "So maybe you could handle Loman. But all it'd take would be one snoop. You don't know how scandals work. You've only been in Washington for little more than half a year. You've got no idea how feeding frenzies get started and how far they can go. And the delight people would take, because of the Sanctity of the Soul —"

"And if I resign my seat? Would anyone give a fart then about my private life?"

Daniel looked pained. "Don't even joke about that!"

"I'm not joking."

The colour drained from Daniel's face. "You promised me." His voice barely exceeded a whisper. "You promised I'd be able to do what I wanted with Josiah's political career. That was the deal, Zeke."

"I'm sorry, Daniel, really I am." Ezekiel crossed the room until he was about a yard from Daniel. "I'd like to give you everything you want, but I can't. Not without erasing every part of me that doesn't fit into a convincing Josiah impersonation. And that's most of me. You wonder why I didn't just go out with you and Jerry? Well the thing is, I'm not interested in having sex with anyone but the other clones. Male or female. I don't know why. And I don't really care why. But that's just how it is. So if you want me to go on being Josiah, you're going to have to make some space for my sexuality. Because there's got to be more to life for me than being a goddamned puppet."

Daniel stared at him for a long time without speaking. Finally, he said, "We can't afford to argue, Zeke. We've got too much at stake. All I ask is that you don't do anything rash. All right?"

Ezekiel appreciated that Daniel negotiated their partnership as cautiously as he did. They both knew that neither of them could afford to ride roughshod over the other. One way or another, Daniel would learn to deal with this.

ABOUT AN HOUR later, standing on the deck outside the sitting room, watching the clones line up in the sand and do push-ups under Loman's direction, Ezekiel wondered idly whether any of them might find the role of Senator Josiah Taylor more agreeable than he did. As they lifted their bodies with the synchronized flow of a Busby Berkeley production number, every one of them different but the same, he felt the memory of that synchronization in his own body, in his muscles and tendons, in his very bones and his blood, and it was almost as though he were down there on the beach working out with them even as he stood up here on the deck, embodying Josiah.

He was still one of them, still the oldest clone. And yet he was also Josiah, for he could see now that he had started to become the man he was impersonating. Somewhere between those two states, though, he was also himself.

Instinct

Joy Parks

I WAS SO NERVOUS on the way to the appointment, I could barely breathe. I kept fingering the piece of paper that held the address, worried that the sweat from my hands might smear it so much that I wouldn't be able to read it. It was stifling inside the dome today, no doubt programmed for one of those unusually hot spring days that take you by surprise. They do that to mimic real weather sometimes. For those who still remember.

I started to touch the paper again, and stopped myself. Feeling the words and numbers on it seemed to calm me. Pens and ink were hard to come by, and lately, I had to be content with watered down dregs of dried ink that I found in the old fountain pen set my aunt had left me. Even the brand name sounded romantic. *Montblanc*. White Mountain. I'd never seen a mountain. Not a real one, anyway. They're too far away and with the oil drought, no one can afford to travel much. I turned the corner onto the street the office was on and pulled out the shred of paper one more time. Match-Tech, 257 7th Avenue, upstairs, 11 AM, April 29, 2045.

Match-Tech's offices were exactly what I'd expected. There were info screens covering every inch of wall in the reception area. They're so common now, it's almost as if they're invisible. I hardly look at them anymore, and barely ever have mine on at home, unless there's a national crisis or something and I might need to know what to do. Funny, someone told me that people used to find lovers online all by themselves, but then they made that illegal. Too many people were arrested for misrepresentation. I'm not even sure how they did it. And of course, my screen has to be on during work hours. I'm a teleresearcher for the archives. But when I'm not working, I usually turn it off. At some point, I realized I didn't need to know every little detail of everything that was happening in the world. Not so much as to want to join a Turnoff group. Not just yet. I'm not that political. I'm just happy for a little quiet now and then, a little space inside my head that's still mine and mine alone. Besides, I like to read books even though they're really hard to find. At least the books I want.

The rest of the room was white, antiseptic white, with a cold blue white light, and chrome and vinyl seats in rows of four bolted to the floor. I had expected that too. But it wasn't the kind of place where you'd expect to find a lover.

Truthfully, I didn't. But there I was anyway.

The receptionist sat in a curved span of white vinyl, a shiny white throne that raised her above the floor, and hid everything but the top of her head from view. After I'd given her my name, she handed me a mobile info screen with more forms to fill out. I'd filled out the main ones at home one night when the loneliness had gotten so strong I could actually feel it following me through the rooms. One of the nights when I couldn't read anymore, when the past I was so drawn to seemed to mock me. It didn't make sense. I was living in a time when all the old stigmas about being a lesbian were gone. An era of perfect equality, everything my foremothers had fought so hard to win. And yet it seemed to me that it might have actually been easier for me to find someone to love when what I am was a forbidden, dangerous, secret. It made me think about how we got this far. I knew the story. Over the years, as each remaining pocket of prejudice disappeared, more and more people began exploring different sexual practices.

Bisexuality became rampant, to the point that not having a few encounters with your own sex was cause for concern. A sign of inflexibility, of inhibition. Even self-loathing. That should have made it easier to find someone, at least for sex, but it didn't. Not for me. I didn't want to be someone's experiment. As more money became available for gender research, reassignments became as common and almost as cheap as a hair cut. MTFs became nu-Women and FTMs became nuMen, which created wave after wave of change and confusion for the GLBT2-SQ community. But we didn't call ourselves that anymore. There were too many of us, with too many different identities. No one could agree on the definitions. So we didn't call ourselves anything. There wasn't any reason to.

The forms were pretty standard. An affidavit attesting to my physical and sexual health. One stating that all the original information I'd given as far as my birth gender, my income, and my dating history were true. A next of kin contact, which I made up. I supposed it was there in case the company was lax in its screening and sent you off to dinner with a cannibalistic axe-murderer. Did they still make axes? I'd only seen them on the info screen.

The receptionist called my name and I stood up. A well-dressed woman with a huge smile on her face beckoned me forward. My expert match consultant, as the company's promotional brochure called her. I'm here, I thought. And I paid in advance.

Forty-five minutes later, my expert match consultant wasn't smiling at all. The best she could muster was an exasperated sigh. None of the profiles of the twenty-five or thirty candidates she'd shown me had caught my interest. A lot of them were obviously nuWomen, even though I'd specifically said I was interested in birth women only. Maybe no one but me could tell the difference anymore. Birth gender was like race and age, it wasn't supposed to matter, and I agree that it shouldn't be an issue for legal things, like jobs and housing. Equal before the law. But when it came to picking a lover, I figured I still had the right to be as discriminating as I wanted to be. The rest of the candidates she showed me seemed too practised, too fake cheery, too woodenly determined to come off as happy, independent, politically correct and exceptional partners. I didn't need exceptional or correct. I wanted someone who would make me feel heat, make me want them, not because they were fine people who were kind to animals or had responsible jobs or voted the same way I did ... but because I couldn't resist them, couldn't get them out of my brain, needed to be near them like I needed water and air. Why was that so hard to understand? I was a lesbian, one of the throwbacks who held on to the term like a life raft. I wanted a woman who'd come into this world as a woman for reasons I couldn't even articulate, and no amount of debate or rationalization was going to change that. Love, sex, passion aren't supposed to be rational, controllable. No matter how lonely it got, I wouldn't allow myself to settle for someone I couldn't be passionate about.

"There are a couple of candidates here from Sanctity City." She smiled. As if we were both in on some private joke.

Hypocrites, I thought. It must be someone who needed adventure in her life. Needed it enough to risk everything. Anyone living in a Sanctity City caught on those lists would probably be banished. If not stoned or burned at the stake or whatever they do inside those gates to make sure no one ever gets out of line. A few years after the Equal Family laws came into being, fundamentalist church groups figured out how they could keep the one born-man, one born-woman marriages safe from what they considered an evil corruption to the sanctity of marriage. And along the way, they figured out a way to make some money doing it. Sanctity Cities sprung up all over the country, like chain stores; housing projects where God-fearing heterosexual families could, for a price beyond the average market value, live in a gated community with others who thought exactly like they did. No gays, lesbians, queers, nuMen or nuWomen could live there. In fact, we couldn't even enter the gates. Which was technically illegal, but the Sanctity City chain had been funded with private money, like private clubs in the past, and they always found ways around the law to keep undesirables out. None of us would have wanted inside anyway.

I shook my head vigorously. True, someone from Sanctity City would at least be a born-woman, physically the kind I was looking for. But I didn't want to be someone's vacation from morality. I wanted someone to fall in love with. And she didn't seem to exist. At least not in Match-Tech's database.

"Please don't be offended, but I have to say that you're one of the more difficult cases we've taken on. Are you sure we can't find a happy compromise?"

The room was getting smaller. I felt like that a lot lately, as if the walls were closing in on me. There wasn't any polite way to answer, so I said nothing. I grabbed my knapsack off the chair beside me and stood up.

She seemed relieved to be rid of me.

"Don't worry, we'll keep looking. We've made our reputation on being able to match up anyone."

I forced a polite nod and told her I'd see myself out.

The waiting room was empty. The receptionist looked up at me, and watched me walk across the room. I could feel her eyes on me. I wondered if she could sense the defeat coming off me. She looked around the room again, almost nervously. Then she motioned me closer.

I walked towards the plastic semi-circle that encased her.

"Are you in a big hurry to get somewhere?" She sounded tough.

"No." I shook my head.

"Then wait for me downstairs. I'll be there in a couple of minutes. I don't want anyone to see us leaving together."

I looked at her, confused.
"Just go."
She urged me on my way with frosted pink nails.
"I'll be there as soon as I can."

I DIDN'T WANT to be conspicuous or too eager about whatever she wanted to talk to me about, so I waited down the block a bit. For a split second, I hoped it wasn't some kind of weird come-on; she wasn't my type at all. But that's not how she had looked at me. Maybe there was some kind of class action against Match-Tech, maybe they took money from desperate lonely people like me and never made a match and she was working inside as a spy. It happened. All I knew was that it was taking her forever.

Finally, she swung out the door, walking fast, and breezed past me, whispering, "Follow me." I did. I followed her down the block, then down a tiny alley where the buildings stretched towards each other like a giant arbor. She looked around again, carefully. She's a spy, I thought. Maybe corporate espionage. On the take with a competitor. Not what I planned, but exciting. Or maybe she was just going to rob me. She felt in her pocket and pulled out a cigarette, thrust it between her lips, looked around again and lit it. Her cheeks hollowed inward as she drew in the smoke. Now I was really nervous. It was illegal to smoke inside the dome. A felony in some parts of the country, stiff penalties, usually jail. I could be in trouble just standing there with her. But it was mesmerizing. The air passing in and out of the O of her lips. In some of the books I'd read, the characters smoked. That was illegal too now, you couldn't show characters smoking or eating restricted foods, like French fries or beef. The tip of the cigarette glowed red. I wondered what it tasted like. What it was like to be addicted to something. To need something so much that you'd be willing to take such a risk.

Finally she spoke. "Match-Tech isn't going to be able to do anything for you. They can't."

I was still watching the smoke. "Why not?" I asked. I knew she was telling the truth.

"I see their databases. Mostly nuWomen, nuMen and rehabilitates. You know, chemical castrations that go either way. And a couple of horny old hags from Sanctity City. No real lesbians."

She blew a stream of smoke straight into my face. It smelled bad, but I liked it. Made me feel dangerous. An outlaw.

"Why? Why no lesbians?"

"I don't know. Maybe they're all matched up. Isn't that what they're like? Maybe they don't have the money. Maybe there aren't any left. I don't know. But they don't come to Match-Tech."

I looked down at my shoes. I'd tried all the other ways to meet someone. This had been my last chance.

She blew more smoke my way. "I can help you. It's pricey. Not just in credits. But I know people."

I looked up at her.

"Are you interested?"

Yes. Yes. Yes, I was interested. I don't know why I trusted this woman who was breaking the law in front of my eyes, taking one last luxurious puff off the cigarette then stamping it out on the ground with the heel of her shoe.

"There's a people-gathering place at the corner of William and First. Be there tonight at seven. They're keeping the skies up later now. Wear something red, they'll find you. You got any family?"

I shook my head. Both my parents had died in the flu pandemic of 2038. I was an only child.

"Just my cat."

She laughed.

"Lesbians and cats. Some things never change. Seven to-night. Wear red." Then she turned and stamped off, into Match-Tech, where there were no real lesbians.

WALKING UP THE street, I realized I was shaking. I was scared. But it was a good fear, not the kind of fear you have of getting sick or losing your job, not the sick-to-your-stomach, how-do-I-fix-this kind of fear. But a fear of the unknown. A fear of being out of routine, of being at the mercy of fate, of not knowing what could happen. I'd never felt like this before.

I walked all the way home and was drenched in sweat when I got there. Natalie Barney Nine lifted herself up off the couch long enough to berate me for not being home at the usual time to feed her. The Nine in her name because she was the ninth clone of the cat I got the year I moved out on my own. At first, people only cloned their pets, to keep familiar loved ones around. Now there were at least a couple of cloning outfits in every decent-sized town. Human Reconstitution Centres, as they were called. In fact, since birthing new children had become so risky, with viruses and new defects being discovered every day, most people just preferred to clone and raise miniature versions of themselves and their partners, generation after generation of parents trying to get it right, on guard for their own bad habits and pitfalls. No surprises.

After I fed Natalie Barney Nine and checked my messages, I stood in the shower for so long I got a warning call from the Water Regulation Office. Red wasn't exactly my colour, but I rooted through the back of my closet and came up with a faded orangey red cardigan that was much too heavy for this time of year. Maybe I could just drape it over my shoulders. It was 5:30

PM and William and First was only about ten minutes away, but I couldn't stay inside any longer. Natalie Barney Nine watched me walk through the apartment suspiciously, as if she knew something was going on. By ten to six, I was out the door. I could pull myself together on the people-gathering bench; I could watch the sundown sim begin. I couldn't stay inside another minute.

"ARE YOU FROM Match-Tech? The one who talked to Carol?"

Carol. That must have been my smoking saviour. I nodded. Seven on the nose. Boy, these people are organized, I thought.

He sat on the edge of the bench, not too close to me, and looked straight ahead. He wore a grey shirt with a hood tied tight around his face and a thin red patterned bandana around his neck. At least I thought it was a "he." I couldn't tell for sure. The voice was low and tempered, but the body hidden beneath the baggy shirt and loose pants was slight. Not a nuMan; the hormones still made you gain weight. It didn't matter. I just wanted to hear what he/she had to say.

"What all did Carol tell you?"

I looked around to see if anyone was watching. I felt like I was in an old spy movie and was ready to deliver the password. The weathermaker was set for a warm spring night. People strolled past slowly in twos and small groups. We seemed to be the only people in the little square who were alone.

"Just that if I wanted to find the match I'm looking for, I should meet you here."

He/she sighed.

"She's got to quit doing that. She keeps sending me people who aren't prepared. It usually turns out to be a waste of time. Most people aren't willing to make the kind of commitment this requires."

Like what, I wondered? What would I have to do? It couldn't
be that bad. I refused to let what little hope I had left be stolen
away so easily. I choked back a tear.

The figure reached up and pulled the hood off. I glanced
sideways. Smooth cheeks and full lips, close cropped dirty blonde
hair. A tiny silver axe with a round blade hung from her ear. Her
ear. I'd seen that symbol before, on the info screen. In my books.
She was a woman after all, maybe even a real lesbian. But there
was no way to know for sure.

"We can't talk here. Let's go somewhere where no one will
notice us."

I stood up on rubbery legs and followed her. Silently we
walked side by side for several blocks, then she turned into a
Caffeine World. I followed her and placed my order. Once we
had our drinks, she motioned for me to pick up a Quiet Mike in
the bin by the counter. Now that public spaces were so large and
the din from so many conversations was so loud, Quiet Mikes
were the only way to have a private conversation in public. We
sat down at a table near the far corner window and adjusted the
headsets to a free frequency, then I clamped the headset to my
ear and swung the microphone around to my mouth.

"You set?"

I nodded and took a good look at her. For someone who had
seemed such a mysterious and foreboding figure in the people-
gathering place, there was nothing scary about her now. Her eyes
were green and wide, her hands smooth as she placed them one
on top of the other on the table like she was settling in for a long
talk between friends. I pushed my mike closer to my lips and
thought about how long it had been since I'd sat across a table
from someone in public.

"So you don't really know why you were asked to meet
me?"

I shook my head. "She … Carol told me that if I wanted

to find the lover I want, I should come to the people-gathering place at seven. And wear red."

She nodded. Her face seemed much softer than it had before.

"Is it you?" I blurted. "I mean, are you the woman she wanted me to meet?"

She broke out into a full smile and shook her head. "No. No it's not me." A bit of pink crept into her cheeks. "But I'm part of an organization that could quite possibly help you find the woman you're looking for. If you're willing to do what's necessary. Like I said before, we ask quite a lot."

"But how do you know what I'm looking for? Who I'm looking for?"

She looked deep into my face.

"Hon, if Carol picked you out, then I know exactly what you're looking for. And I hate to break it to you, but she's not easy to find."

Hon.

I loved the sound of that word. The way it hung between us, softening the blow of what she had said. No one used terms of endearment like that anymore. It was too easy to be sued for emotional harassment.

"Why? Why is it so hard?"

She drummed her fingers on the table. "Because they couldn't leave well enough alone."

"Who?" I asked. I didn't know what she meant.

She motioned to the people sitting around us.

"Us. Them. Everyone. They figured if they couldn't stop us or shut us up, then they'd do the next best thing. They'd find a way to control us and we wouldn't even know we were being controlled, being assimilated, having our power, our difference taken away. We'd mistake it for acceptance, for achieving some sort of goal that most of us had forgotten we'd ever wanted in the first place. But we'd go along because it had to be right, to be equal. To be the same. But equal doesn't mean the same. And by the time we'd figured out what was really going on, we were done for. They finally got it right. All those years of hating us had only made us stronger. But it took only a couple of decades of acceptance to make us disappear."

She was getting more and more agitated and I didn't know what she meant. I was alone on a closed circuit mike with a stranger who was getting really angry. That's just not safe. Anger is bad. Unproductive. For a moment, I was sorry I had come at all. I didn't want her to turn that anger on me. I didn't understand what she meant. But still … I could feel it. A sadness stirring up in me that I just couldn't place. A pining for something I'd never had.

"What disappeared?" But I had a sense I knew the answer.

"Us. You. Me. Lesbians. Dykes. Fags. Queers. The community. Hell, even the trannies were more real back when you actually had to have some real motivation for jumping the gender line. Not like now, when you get the operation easier than you could once get a pack of smokes. All gone now."

I looked around to make sure no one had heard her.

I started to protest. It felt like I was reciting something I'd learned in school. "But there are so many of us now. I read a study. More than half of the population has had – or plans to have – sex with their own gender. And no one but those who live in Sanctity Cities is prejudiced against us anymore. They can't be. It's illegal. We finally got what generations had been working for. We achieved full equality."

"No. That's not what we got." She banged her fist on the table. People stared from the tables around us. I hunched closer to her.

"We got fashionable. We got popular. Look, there are tons of people who sleep with their own sex. And there are plenty of people who play at gender … and maybe some of them really don't fit the body they were born into. Who knows anymore? But we've become the same as everyone else. We've lost our instincts. How can you survive without instincts? Take gaydar, for instance. That was real, you know … and you needed it back then. To figure people out. To not get slapped or arrested. Or killed. It made us special. It's evolved right out of us. Bet you thought I was male, didn't you? And there's no community. We're too fractured. We're everywhere … and nowhere. It's a whole new way of being invisible."

She was quiet for a moment.

"Accepted. We weren't accepted, my dear, we were obliterated." She sighed. "I'm sorry … I can't do any more of this tonight. Do you still want to go on? Find out what we can do for you?"

I looked at her. The anger had left her and she looked limp and tired. She was older than I had first realized.

"I'm … I'm lonely."

That sounded pathetic and I thought I was going to burst into tears right there.

Her face softened. "Give me your address."

She didn't pull out a beamer, so I felt in my pocket for a scrap of paper and a bit of pencil. She looked impressed.

"I'll come to you tomorrow night. Seven sharp."

And then she was gone.

I DON'T REMEMBER walking home. I didn't sleep at all that night, and the next day was the longest I'd ever had to get through. That includes the time a couple of years ago when the dome went on the fritz and they couldn't get the sun to set for nearly a week. A lot of people had to go into stress camps then. I turned on my work info screen and tried to deal with some minor research requests, but I couldn't concentrate. I knew I couldn't get away with outing the screen until at least four without a good excuse. Finally, the hour came and I could stop pretending to work. I logged out and lay on my bed staring up at the ceiling. I tried to eat, but every bite sat like lead in my stomach.

The auto-concierge screen lit up at exactly seven.

She was wearing the same grey hood and loose pants when she showed up at my door. She looked nervous. Once inside, she lifted her hood and slipped the whole thing off, revealing a slight but solid body encased in a tight long-sleeved black T-shirt. I offered to make some tea, mostly so I'd have something to do, and she accepted. When I walked back into the sitting room, she was looking through the books on my shelves, running a finger down their spines. Natalie Barney Nine was padding beside her, watching her every move. That made me feel better. I trust a cat's instinct far more than my own.

Finally, I brought in the tea. She sat back on the couch and looked almost comfortable. I realized that I didn't know her name, but it didn't feel right to ask. I sat in the armchair across from her and waited.

"So. You want to know more?" She sipped her tea.

I nodded.

"Okay, I'll try to stop editorializing. Besides, there are enough books about our history on those shelves that I should be able to gloss over some of the facts." She cleared her throat.

"You would have been very young when the Equal Family laws were put in place. I was with a group that worked to get same-sex marriage legalized. So when it all finally became legal, not just here and there, in Canada, in Holland, but everywhere, we were ecstatic. It was the culmination of every hope and desire and dream of just about every activist, from Stonewall and before. We believed we had achieved full and total equality, and that through this, we would basically eradicate any form of oppression over sexual preference."

"Didn't you?" I asked.

She pursed her lips.

"It seemed that way for a while. And there were other things that contributed. Medical research was making gender reassignment day surgery safer and less expensive. The laws that dealt with binary gender were rewritten. And that raised a lot of questions. If you are born a woman, become a nuMan and still want women, does that make you straight? There were no clear answers. And it didn't seem to matter at the time. Now we know better. Human Reconstitution ... we still called it cloning back then ... was making it possible for lesbians and gay men to have and raise their own children, without help from the opposite sex. We thought we had it made."

I nodded. I was sitting across from a woman who'd made history. And seemed to regret it.

She put her cup on the table, and leaned forward towards me. "Then a couple of us started noticing that it wasn't all what we'd expected. There was nothing different about us anymore, no reason to congregate, no gay bars, no dyke potlucks, no gay media. Nothing to set us apart, nothing to call our own. We weren't oppressed anymore ... we just weren't there anymore. A lot of gay men and lesbians had decided to pack it in and become nuMen and nuWomen. And they abandoned what was left of the community. We couldn't blame them. But we missed them."

I was fascinated. I'd never heard anyone talk about the Great Assimilation as if it were a bad thing.

"But everyone got more open about his or her sexuality. There was no stigma to sleeping with your own sex. Or changing gender. How could that be a bad thing?"

She looked at me and smiled sadly.

"Yeah, they really played up the sex part. You know, that's not all it takes to make someone a lesbian. Or gay. Or transgender. A lot of people learned too late that changing your genitals doesn't make you something else. They still didn't feel accepted. They couldn't change what was in their heads. And you should know … a woman can sleep with a dozen women and that doesn't mean she's a lesbian. Just like being married to a man doesn't make you straight. Look at all those poor miserable women in Sanctity City. You saw them at Match-Tech. Being a lesbian is here." She touched her heart. "Not here." She gestured between her legs.

She was quiet for a moment. Then seemed to get her second wind.

"A few of us started to see what full assimilation had done to us. Especially those of us who'd never really been comfortable with the whole monogamy, white picket fence, till death do us part deal. And we realized how wrong we had been. That instead of working to become the same as everyone else, we should have put that energy and time and effort into demanding respect for being just as we were. Different. And wonderful."

I nodded. Different. Wonderful. There was something about those words together that made me feel sad.

"We decided to do something about it. So we started buying up cheap bits of land outside domed cities."

"You can't live out there," I blurted. The ozone. The air quality. I didn't want to be sent outside the dome to die.

She grinned.

"There's nothing wrong with the air outside the domes. Or the water. They found a way to fix the ozone about six years after the last dome went in. Once the domes went up and the garbage and toxics were disposed of inside, the water problems went away too. The same technology used to genetically modify foods also enables plants to clean the air at a rate twenty-five times that of a normal tree. It's fine out there."

I was shocked. I didn't believe her. "But … why? Why doesn't anyone know that?"

"Because they don't want you to leave. They want you to live here, like this. Never travel, work at home, stay at home, isolated. Nothing to do but shop and watch the sunset sims and maybe stop at Caffeine World every now and then. Travel makes you see how others live and fills you with questions. And when people get together, they talk. They plan. They make change. They revolt. That doesn't happen now."

"Who are they?"

"The usual suspects. The government. The media. Now mostly the corporations. They need you to stay right where you are. And keep living exactly as they tell you. The corporations loved the Assimilation. More joint-income households, more consumers. How do you think they managed to get the votes they needed to change the laws?"

I'd never heard anyone say things like this before. I didn't know if she was lying. But crazy as it sounded, I wanted to believe her. Because if what she said was true, then it wasn't just me.

She continued.

"So, like I said, we bought land, we urban-formed cities. A lot of us didn't fit here anymore and the only way to live as we knew how was to do it outside of the domes. To build communities where we could live gay and lesbian and transgendered lives as we wished. Not as the rest of the world would have us."

"And I can go there? To one of these communities? I could find a lover there? A real lesbian?" I couldn't hide the excitement rising in my voice.

"You could find a whole life to love there. But … there are consequences. All real choices have consequences."

I sat back and took a deep breath and asked her what that meant.

"You have to give up everything you have here. You have to slip away unnoticed. You're an only child and an orphan, so that part is easier for you. You can take the cat. A few personal effects. Some books maybe. But that's it. And you leave everything to us. We dispose of your property and use the money we make to help fund the work we do. We make all the arrangements, do all the work. You just give us the information we need, and do what we tell you to do."

"To where?" She had said it was outside the dome. I wondered how far.

"To wherever you want. Actually, to whenever you want." She smiled like it was a riddle. I looked perplexed enough to make her continue.

"We realized that life as a lesbian meant different things at different times. You read Faderman, right? I saw it on your shelf. So you know what I mean. Some of us felt more comfortable, more a part of the community at different times. So we've tried to accommodate that. You get to pick the period in lesbian herstory that appeals to you the most. Honestly, after the nineties, there really weren't historically distinct eras anyway. Everything was a mish-mash of retro this and that."

I thought it sounded wonderful. Like one of those old-fashioned reality TV shows. But they didn't make you leave and it never ended.

She fished a stack of photos out of her pockets and spread them on the table.

"I have a women's commune in the seventies. All organic farming and such. But you keep saying 'a' lover. Those weren't exactly the years to be monogamous."

I grinned and told her just one would be fine.

She turned over another deck of photos. "What about the

mid-eighties? They were interesting. That's when we started thinking about sex again."

She watched me look at the photos. The women looked tense, like they were trying too hard to smile. But the clothes were fun. Much more so than now. Short skirts and tiny tight sleeveless shirts that showed off hard girl arm muscles.

"There's the nineties too. Are you interested in being a mother? If so, that's the time I'd pick."

More photos. Smiling women, dancing women, couples and groups and a lot of women without clothes dancing and swaying in a field where more women were playing music. Michigan, she had called it. But I was starting to feel hopeless again. Not a part of any of this. While the women were women, and looked like they were living interesting lives, I still didn't feel how I thought I'd feel. There was still no … heat. No one I couldn't live without.

There was an unexpected noise outside on the street. Natalie Barney Nine jumped down off the top of the couch and knocked a stack of photos across the floor. I bent over to help pick them up and looked down at the one in my hand. A faint moan escaped my lips.

"Where is she from?" I asked. "When?"

She frowned at me, held out her hand to take the photos. "That … you don't want that. That's something else altogether."

But I did. I did want this. And I knew it immediately. Nothing had ever felt as right as this photo. It was obviously taken in a place where people gathered. There were glasses on the table and most of the women had cigarettes in their hands. For a moment, I thought of Carol, who brought me to the point I am now. In the middle of the photo was the one who caught my eye. Her short dark hair was slicked back, shiny. I wanted to touch it. Her eyes shone dark; she was smirking almost, like she knew a secret. Her elbows were firm on the table … and she had turned her chair backwards to straddle it, feet flat on the floor on either side. Her arms were firm. Her hands were large but graceful. And while there was nothing girlish about her, I knew this was no nuMan in waiting, this was still a woman, a different kind of woman. One who understood how different women can be. How free and rebellious and strong. I felt a shiver. A flutter through my gut.

"No, I want this … I want her."

She sighed. She took the photo and turned it over.

"We're talking no protection at all now. No laws. No rights. Nothing. Just a couple of divey bars to hang out in on streets most people wouldn't walk on after dark. And relationships that usually don't last. Can't last. And women who get mistaken for men or called freaks. You could get arrested then if you weren't wearing the right clothes."

I'd read about that. Three pieces of women's clothing. The trick was to sew lace trim on cotton sport socks. Why did I remember that? I didn't care. My heart was still racing.

"And you'll have to sign a special disclaimer saying I warned you. No offence, but only special cases go here. And there's no coming back from this one. Too difficult."

"Wait a minute … if we created it, why are there such problems? Where's the homophobia coming from?"

I'd never said that word aloud before. I'd never heard it spoken.

"Volunteers. Those who felt crowded out by the equality laws. Those who wanted to go back to the 'good old days'. Not so different than you. What, you think they just made some laws and all the hate went away? Not a chance."

I winced.

"I know, it's sad and it seems strange that we'd re-create that too. But the anger always has to go somewhere, and we had to keep it authentic. Otherwise, why bother? How do you live as a rebel if there's nothing to rebel against?"

"Do they get recruited like you recruited me?'"

She took a long time to answer.

"Yes, I guess. No. Honestly, I don't know the details. Better that way, I think. I have enough to worry about. I can pretty much imagine where they find them. There are still a couple of underground bars just outside the fringe of most cities. I don't want to think of what goes on in them. Usually it's men, but not always, and mostly the kind that got crowded out of things, when it took more than a loud voice, white skin, and some upper body strength to get by. And sometimes it's just tourists from some Sanctity City or another who want a weekend trip...."

She looked at me, as if she were searching my face to see if I was content with her answer. To see if I was frightened enough to change my mind.

"Look," she continued, "most of my transports have been women like you. Women who were looking for something ... someone ... who can't exist here and now. Women who made the decision to go out of love. Or at least the possibility of it. The others. They have different reasons. They want to reclaim the dominance they used to have, the power. They feel weak here because they aren't in control anymore. But they're here just the same and I don't think they'd be all that hard to find. Those kind always had a way of seeking each other out. I guess that's one of the few things we had in common with them. And the truth is, they're just as dangerous here and now as they were in the time you're going to. Maybe even more so now because we pretend they don't exist. And we don't have the defences we used to have."

My mouth felt dry. "Does anything ever happen? Do people...."

"Things happen. People get hurt. We can't control anything once you get there. I told you that. There are risks. But you learn how to deal. Your instincts will kick in. In the past, there were always risks to being different. You know that, you're read all about it."

I stroked Natalie Barney Nine and thought about it. If that kind of hatred still existed here, just not openly, then I really wasn't any safer here than I was where … when I wanted to go. The only difference was now I was aware of it.

"And there's no cloning."

My hand tensed around Natalie Barney Nine's underbelly. Nine. Nine lives is normal for a natural-born cat. That's what they used to say. Besides, she was still a kitten. I'd cross that bridge when I came to it.

I knew I didn't belong here. I didn't know where I belonged. Maybe it wouldn't work out. But I'd be no worse off than now. No lonelier. "I'll sign," I said, like I was making an announcement.

I could tell she knew there was no talking me out of it.

"Remember. We don't exist after you land. You never talk about it."

Before she left that night, I signed the papers. Her instructions were simple. Over the course of the next few days, I was to pack a small bag of things I wanted to take, personal items only. Nothing electronic. Nothing that could be tracked. I would receive an extensive questionnaire over my private info screen that I was to complete and send back as soon as possible. I was to keep working as usual, shop for food, be seen by my neighbours. And I was not to speak a word of my plans to anyone.

THAT NIGHT when I slipped into bed, I felt fresh and new. The image of the dark-haired woman burned in my mind, spread the heat out through my body. I couldn't remember when I felt so … alive. So needy. I thought of her strong arms, and drew my hand down below my sheet to find myself soaking wet between my legs.…

The questionnaire arrived the next morning. More than four hundred questions, right down to my clothing sizes and favourite foods. The kind of women I was attracted to. I kept sneaking time away from work during the day to finish it and sent it off that night.

Then there was nothing left to do but pack. And wait.

The next night, I cleaned my unit, threw out anything I didn't want strangers to find, and put Natalie Barney's carrying case by the door. If anyone saw it, I could say she had an appointment with the vet. I put some family photographs, a few pieces of jewelry my mom had given me, some underwear, and a change of clothes in the bag. It wasn't even half full. I went to my bookshelves and gently wrapped three very old volumes that had been good friends to me. Lillian Faderman's *Odd Girls and Twilight Lovers*. Ann Bannon's *Beebo Brinker*. *The Swashbuckler* by Lee Lynch. Books I loved for the way they spoke about our history. I had a feeling they'd come in handy now where … when … I was going.

I kept waiting to have second thoughts. To panic, to go to Match-Tech and call it off. But it didn't happen. It had been almost a week since I'd signed the papers. I was beginning to worry that they'd forgotten about me.

But two nights later, it happened. There was a buzz at the door around one-thirty in the morning. I checked the info screen and saw the familiar grey hood. It was her. It was time. My stomach leaped and my mouth went dry. I thought I'd be afraid. But instead I was excited. And determined.

A voice informed me I had ten minutes.

I grabbed Natalie Barney Nine off the bed and slipped her into the case. Dumped her food and water dishes and shoved them in my bag. I threw a sweater over my shoulders, turned off the lights, and left. I didn't look behind. There was a vehicle outside, a rogue one, not fitted with the tiny wheels that keep cars on their tracks. Not allowed. She was standing behind the car, looking nervous. As usual. I wondered how many times she'd done this. Natalie Barney Nine meowed as I ran across the road. The woman in grey took the cat case and my bag and motioned me into the vehicle.

It was dark inside, and quiet, aside from Natalie Barney rustling around trying to figure out what was going on. There were two hooded figures in front, one driving, the other looking out the window. No one said a word. It was like I wasn't there.

We rounded corners and turned down one street after another. That explained why it was rogue. It felt odd to be in a car and not restricted to the track, not hearing the clang of metal on metal, just the smooth hum of the engine. We'd driven for some time when I realized that we were outside the dome. And I was still breathing. She was right. Nothing looked dangerous out here, just a few boarded-up buildings. And the odd house lights of outfringers. People really did live out here.

We drove for another twenty minutes through the pitch-black night when finally she turned to me.

"Are you ready?"

I nodded, too nervous to speak. Then realized she couldn't see much of me in the darkened car and managed to squeak out a yes.

"There's something we have to do to assure everyone's safety. I promise it won't hurt a bit."

She held an injection plunger in one hand and held the other out to take my hand. I felt like I was in a trance. I absent-mindedly petted Natalie Barney through the case as if I was going away for a while, and then surrendered my hand.

That was the last thing I remembered.

* * *

WHEN I WOKE up, it was dark outside. I looked down. Natalie Barney Nine was cuddled against my feet. Perfectly normal. There was a dim light on in what appeared to be the hall outside the room; I could see enough to switch on the light on the bedside table. The room lit up and I smiled. There was a lovely brass bed, just like the ones I'd seen in antique books ... and a dresser and a vanity table and a tiny closet.

I got up and walked into the hall and I could see the entire apartment from where I stood. A railroad apartment, rooms in a row, connected by doors. I remembered reading about them. Joan Nestle, in her stories about New York, about Greenwich Village in the fifties.

There was food in the fridge and cat food in the cupboard.

According to the material left on the desk, I am Anne. I'm supposed to be from Seattle. And I moved to the Village after I graduated from college. I have a job reading manuscripts for a small publishing company that specializes in history. I like that. I'm starting to understand why they asked all those questions.

I look out the window. I've never seen so many lights. No power drought here. I never go out at night. But everything has changed. I've changed too and I want to go exploring. See what's out there. If she's out there. I shower and sit at the vanity. There's a hairbrush and some perfume, which I've never used before. I couldn't. All those Personal Scent laws. It smells like vanilla and cinnamon and roses and fresh grass. I unfold the stockings that lie on the vanity table; they feel like fog on my legs. I slip into the tight straight black skirt that hangs in the closet. I love the way it cups my ass, and how the heels someone has left waiting for me stretch my calves. I've never felt like this before. Never knew I wanted to. How could they know when I didn't? There's a deep mauve twin set in my closet, it's cashmere, I've read about that too ... and it feels sleek and warm against my skin. I bend down in front of the mirror and sweep the lipstick over my lips.

Revlon's Cherries in the Snow. My skin lights up. My mouth is like a bow. I've never done this before, never, ever, and yet I know what to do, and it all feels so right. Instincts, she had said that night at Caffeine World. Seemed like a long time ago. She said we needed to follow our instincts. And I do.

I call out to Natalie Barney Nine, who had made a nest of the sheets, and pick up my handbag, which holds a few dollars, my apartment keys and another lipstick, in the same rosy red, attached to a tiny mirror. The leather is so soft and rich. I've never carried one of these before, but it feels right, the strap in my hand swinging as I walk. I start for the door, for the street, to look for her, the woman in the photo, the women like her, the women who make my heart beat. The kind of woman I can't live without. I've come a long way but I know what it will take to find her.

I'll just follow my instincts.

The Chosen Few

Caro Soles

THE MERLIN PANEL shimmered, sending out waves of dimpled colour around the imprint of Liam's hand.

"This is bullshit." He started to pull his hand away, but Jamal's large black fingers pushed it back against the wall.

"Come on, man. You gotta go first. Don't be a chickenshit." The others immediately began to crow and cluck, flapping their arms, an animated khaki chorus.

"All right, all right! Bring it on!" Far from being upset by the ribbing, Liam saw it as a sign of acceptance.

The Cobras hadn't been together long. They were hand-picked, an elite group, some gay, some straight, part of Attack Squadron 388. It was the first time openly gay soldiers had made it into a marine wing group since the new policy had opened the doors four years earlier. Some, like Liam and his lover Jack, were back from serving in the Aladdin Offensive. Some had come from other units or were recruited from other bases. They had all been through a grueling six-week training period in the latest in weaponry and fold wing aircraft at Fort Eisler, the marine base in California, and tonight they were celebrating. Everyone had made it one step closer to the top secret mission that had been the gossip of the base for weeks.

"Merlin wasn't a fortune teller, you know," Jack pointed out, balancing another sugar cube on top of the pyramid he was building.

"Yeah, yeah, who cares?" Jamal stuffed a wad of gum in his mouth and settled back in his chair.

Rachel poured more rum in her glass. "So ask already! Who's going to make the final cut?"

"He can't ask about anyone but himself," Boomer said, tossing back a handful of peanuts. "That's the rules."

"There are rules?" Jack said. "Who knew?"

Liam pulled his hand away from the glowing panel to cuff his boyfriend on the head playfully, then placed his palm in exactly the same spot.

"You are strong-willed and highly competitive, with much leadership potential," Merlin intoned suddenly.

"Yadda, yadda," muttered Jamal. "He's the great white hope of the rainbow nation."

"It's just getting stuff from his file based on his palm print, you know," Jack murmured.

"Dark clouds are gathering," Merlin's robotic voice continued. "Hold close those you love."

"Not in front of me," cried Boomer.

"Get over it, you arrogant het." Rachel punched him none too gently on the bicep.

"Danger surrounds you," Merlin's voice went on, impervious to the catcalls and jeers that greeted this latest announcement. "Curb your impulses. Things are not what they seem."

"Will I get picked to go on the TOP SECRET MISSION?" Liam asked, his voice deep and dramatic.

There was silence as they all waited for the answer.

"You are to fly among the eagles. Listen to their call only." The colours on the Merlin panel flickered then faded away, leaving nothing but the dull grey wall of the lounge. Liam withdrew his hand.

"Pile of crap," he said.

"I dunno." Jamal patted his new moustache with one finger. "He said you're goin', right?"

"Yeah," sneered Boomer. "The politically correct choice."

"Nope." Rachel pushed her glass away and stood up. "He said 'fly with the eagles,' which I take to mean the Eagle Squad, not this mission. I gotta go. See ya."

"Hah, what does she know," muttered Ramon, the youngest member of the group, watching Rachel make her way to the door with evident dislike.

Liam gazed steadily at Jack as though he were the only one at the table. "The Eagle Squad is gathering intel on the Ekvanistan Nations in the Balkans," he said.

"We should just drop a bomb on the fucking Ekies and get it over with," Squint said, his words not quite slurring yet. "They've been nothing but trouble for years, stirring up the entire eastern sector like they do, claiming to be religious and all."

"No way I'll be ordered to join the Eagles any time soon," Liam went on, ignoring Squint. "I'll be picked for this mission. We both will."

Jack shook his head. "You have seniority and more combat experience than me."

"Bullshit!" Liam thumped the table with his fist. "You're a weapons expert with higher scores on the last Dar-Fischer tests than me."

"If you two are gonna fight, I'm outta here," Jamal said.

"Me too," said Boomer. "It's embarrassing, right, Ramon?"

"We're not fighting," Liam and Jack said in unison.

Everyone laughed. Ramon, uncertain of the undercurrents, grinned nervously and ordered another round.

* * *

SOMETHING BIG was in the air. Raw recruits had been pouring in for basic training, more shipped to other marine bases or airlifted out to God knows where. No one was talking. The Cobras had been special from the start, and now that the brass was looking for a chosen few for some new mission, it seemed obvious the chosen would come from this wing group, or at least their squad. Just how many were needed, no one was sure. As the group grew more at ease with each other, they compared notes and the intel they had been able to gather, trying to piece together what the brass was looking for. Did it matter if you were married? Male? Female? Straight? Gay? Special sniper skills? Combat experience? Underwater training? Their group included all of the above. They knew they were being watched, tested, graded according to some esoteric scale. But now the training was over. Surely they would find out soon who had been picked?

"We're going to be separated," Jack said gloomily to the others as they met in the storeroom near M barracks later that night. It was hard to find any sort of privacy on the base and they had to be especially careful. Being out and proud was all very well on paper, but attitudes don't change overnight. The ruling was still new and they didn't want to be a test case.

"They're picking the best, Jack. That's us."

"You, yes. You're an experienced pilot, a First Lieutenant, even have a medal or two. Me? I'm just a –"

"Stop putting yourself down! You're a weapons specialist, first class, and you have combat experience too. Have you forgotten how we met?"

Jack laughed. "Yeah. You came flying through a window in front of an exploding shell in that hell-hole town with the unpronounceable name."

"Best jump I ever made!"

"First time you jumped my bones, that's for sure," Jack said.

They stopped talking, hearing footsteps outside the door.

"Why would the brass pick gays anyway?" Jack whispered.

"They want the place redecorated?"

"Could certainly use it," Jack said, looking around.

"Stop worrying," Liam said, slipping an arm around his shoulders. But he was worried, too. This mission was important to them, a chance to prove themselves, a chance for real glory and recognition and a big boost to their careers. Liam had his eyes on a Captain's bars.

BUT NEXT MORNING, his dream lay shattered like broken glass. He looked at the message on his PDA in disbelief. Negative! He hadn't made it after all. Hubris, he thought. He had been so sure. Everyone had been so sure! What had gone wrong? The results were supposed to be secret, but no military rule could stop the gossip mill. Within an hour Liam knew that Jack, Squint, and Boomer had been picked, and Rachel, Ramon, and Jamal would stay behind. As he moved numbly through the routine of his day, everyone assumed Liam was going and he neither confirmed nor denied their covert winks and nudges.

The more time passed, the harder it was to admit the truth, even to himself. How could he tell Jack? He dreaded the evening when the Cobras would gather for their farewell drink. Would the others see him as the failure he saw himself? Some part of his brain knew how illogical he was being, but it made no difference. When he thought of Jack going without him, he felt a wrench of loss so strong it was a physical pain in his gut. He couldn't lose him now!

The day dragged on. Bit by bit, information filtered through to him. He was wading through some hated paperwork when he received a message from Jack that the group was leaving at

1500 hours. Forty-five minutes! They were obviously trying to do this with no fuss. He thrust the files back in their folders, flung them into the desk, and rushed off to find Jack. He had no idea what he was going to say, but at the very least they had to work out the code they could use to communicate. In a harsh military environment, where they were denied conjugal rights, where a big step forward was just to be accepted at all, text messages, instant photos, and a few stolen moments in the storeroom got them through.

Jack wasn't responding to messages. Liam checked his bunk and their usual haunts. No one had seen him. Time was running out. He headed for the storage room near Barracks M.

As he opened the door, the smell hit him. Deep retching noises echoed off the metal walls. "Jack? Jack!" He rushed forward, alarm flooding his brain. But it wasn't Jack he found but Boomer, crouched on all fours on the metal floor. The big Cajun pulled himself away from Liam's arms and threw up again onto a crate of gun casings.

"Shit. We'd better get you an ambulance," Liam said.

"No! Don't tell them…" He stopped, gasping for breath, his face grey and slick with sweat. He was so weak he could barely hold his head up. Drool dribbled from one corner of his mouth. He seemed shrunken inside his uniform. Around his neck was the electronic ID card identifying him as one of those chosen for the mission, its holographic insignia glinting in the dim light.

They'll need a replacement, Liam thought. He glanced at his watch. It wouldn't be possible now to contact the number of people necessary to change Boomer's name for his on the crew list, would it? Boomer. He didn't even know the man's real name. Twice he had caught him knocking back painkillers by the handful. Jack had talked him out of reporting the guy, even though he was one of the few in the unit who let the odd homophobic remark slip out. Boomer had been injured at Jumbalya four months ago and the pain still ruled him. Had he taken too much? Mixed some deadly cocktail to chase the pain demons before embarking on the mission?

Liam pulled out his PDA and accessed the medic alert number. Something made him pause.

"Don't tell..." Boomer tried to reach out to stop him but didn't have the strength.

Don't ask, don't tell. The outdated phrase echoed in Liam's mind. "You're burning up," he said, touching Boomer's forehead. "What did you take?"

"Just a little somethin' to take the edge off." Boomer opened his hand and an unmarked pill bottle spilled out.

"You fucking asshole," muttered Liam, furious that this druggie had been chosen instead of him. "What the hell was in there?"

"What do you care? Whadda... fuck...." Boomer's eyes flickered, then rolled up in his head. The big man slipped sideways, slowly crumpling to the floor.

Liam stood looking down at him, his brain racing with possibilities. At last he reached down and felt for a pulse. There was one, but it was faint.

"Fuck." He slid the ID key from around Boomer's neck, pocketed the man's PDA and left, closing the door softly behind him.

Back at his own bunk, he hurriedly packed his duffle, throwing things in helter skelter, not giving himself time to think. If things went according to schedule, he could just make it to the assembly point spelled out in Boomer's PDA. Everyone expected him to be there. With any luck, no one would do more than a head count. But when he got to the heliport, Jeep tires spinning on the wet ground as the rain closed in, the main copter had already left. Three other servicemen arrived at the same time, running over to huddle with him under the shelter of Hangar Two. He had seen them around the base but didn't know them.

"If it ain't the homo hero," the tall one muttered under his breath.

"You with C.S.U., sir?" the redhead asked, wiping rain off his face.

Liam nodded.

"What'll we do? Call the brass?"

"Not necessary." Liam outranked them, thank God, since the last thing he wanted was someone checking the passenger list. Ramon, he thought suddenly. The boy would do anything for him. But jeopardize his career? "I guess I'll find out," he muttered, punching in an urgent message to Ramon on his PDA.

Five minutes later the young man appeared, clutching two chopper key cards. "Come on, sir." He motioned them to the next hangar. "I can fly a Hawk Nine through any storm. No sweat."

Bless the corps for training marines to obey without question, Liam thought, following the young man. This was something that had always given him problems. The chopper looked threatening, hovering above them on the damp asphalt. "Are you sure you can make it out to the ship and back in this thing? It's pretty far out and the weather's getting worse."

"Just tell me where."

"USS aircraft carrier *Phoenix*."

"Never heard of it. Co-ordinates?"

Liam read them off.

"Piece of cake." Ramon jumped into the copter. His hands blurred over the instrument panel as he went through the take-off routine. Liam heaved his duffle inside and climbed up after the others, his nerves singing with tension. "Can't you go any faster?" he snapped.

Ramon's dark eyes looked back at him reproachfully. All he said was, "Fasten your seatbelt."

* * *

THE RIDE SEEMED to take forever. Liam had been right about the weather, and just as they left land behind, the wind picked up fiercely and rain gushed out of the sky. The sea, barely visible beneath them, heaved into high peaks like mountains. The other three seemed unconcerned. They ignored him, joking among themselves as the rain pounded against metal all around them. Liam kept seeing Boomer's body slumped over on the cement floor, drool hanging out of one corner of his mouth. And him, doing nothing to help. Thinking only of himself, and Jack. Or was it raw ambition that let the man die at his feet? If he was dead....

BY THE TIME they landed on the *Phoenix*, he was so stiff with tension he could barely climb down the ladder. The wind was howling now and he had to shout to make himself heard. For one wild moment the way back to the safety of the base beckoned as he gazed at Ramon's anxious face hanging out of the cockpit. But he hadn't gotten this far by taking the safe road. He returned Ramon's salute and hurried through the torrents of rain into the ship with the others. The vessel shuddered and pitched in the weather, lurching against the sickening swell.

The mission ship was a surprise. Its size was impressive but it felt neglected. No one greeted them, no security questioned who they were. Grey paint peeled from the walls in the narrow corridors. The brick-red floor was faded from so many years.

"Not exactly ship-shape, is she?" muttered the redhead.

Just as they had given up on a welcoming committee, a young seaman appeared and greeted them with a sketchy salute.

"You're late, sir," he said, his voice high and strained in the wind. "Follow me. I'll take you to your quarters."

He guided them down another corridor, through a door and into a long dormitory of bunks three deep. Liam's companions stayed there, while he was ushered to the end, to one of the tiny cells reserved for the junior officers. While he stowed his duffle in the footlocker, the sailor started to copy Boomer's name, rank, and serial number onto the card on the door.

"Wait. The ID cards must have gotten mixed up," Liam said, showing his dog tags. The seaman made out a new card without question, slipped it on the door, and left.

Liam felt a new rush of energy as he watched the young man disappear. Protocol would mean reporting for duty to the Captain, but he had to see Jack first. If they were going to discipline him, he needed the picture of his lover's smile of welcome to take with him to the brig.

Jack wasn't answering his messages so Liam checked the other cards along the corridor. Jack's name wasn't among them.

"Looking for your boyfriend?" one of his travelling companions asked as he squeezed by.

Liam stopped and gave him a long look. "Looking for your boyfriend, *sir*," he said.

The smile disappeared from the kid's face.

"Sorry, sir," he mumbled.

As Liam continued his search, he noticed the usual surveillance cameras everywhere, but no one hailed him or questioned who he was or where he was going. Was no one monitoring the place, now that they were out to sea, heading for their strike target? Where was the crew?

As he emerged onto Deck C, a voice finally challenged him over the ship's speaker system. But it wasn't the Captain he was ordered to report to. It was the First Officer. Strange, he thought. A young ensign arrived at that moment and he followed the girl to the officer's ready room. She opened the door, announced him, and withdrew.

"You fucking idiot!" thundered the man behind the desk.

"*Davey?*" Liam stared at the red-faced man who was once long ago his lover.

"Don't you Davey me, you stupid bastard!"

"Well, don't fall all over me with kisses, Commander," Liam said, but a cold shiver started down his spine.

"Moron!" Davey slumped back in his big leather chair and covered his face with one big hand. "Sit down."

Liam sank into the only other chair in the cabin. Davey looked older, much older, than when they had first met. Liam had been nineteen when he encountered Davey Lindstrom in a bar in Atlanta. The place was off the beaten track, and Liam was working part-time to supplement his college money. It was lust at first sight for both, but the older man feared for his career if their affair became known. Davey was already an officer with a lot to lose. But that was ten years ago, at least. Why all this anger? It seemed far too extreme for what he had done, surely? Or at least for what Davey thought he had done. For an instant, Boomer's sweat-soaked face flashed into his mind's eye and he winced.

"You always were an impulsive S.O.B."

"I thought that was one of my more endearing characteristics," Liam said.

"Asswipe." Davey shifted his weight and gazed at the row of monitors lining the wall to Liam's right. Storage holds filled with weaponry and stretches of narrow empty corridors flickered on the screens.

Liam studied the full face he had once known so well, the generous mouth, the unruly iron-grey hair that refused to lie flat. The normally bright blue eyes were dull with exhaustion, and there was a drained, pinched look around his nose that had never been there before.

Liam leaned forward, his elbows on his knees. "What's going on here, Davey?"

The other man shifted again and sighed. "You've really stepped in it this time," he said at last. "I don't know what stupid stunt you pulled to get here and I don't want to know."

"If I wasn't here, you'd be a man short," Liam said.

"I wish we were."

"Look, it's obvious you don't want me here, for some personal reasons I can't begin to fathom. I should be talking to the Captain anyway." Liam got to his feet.

"The Captain blew his brains out four hours ago. I'm in charge."

Liam sat down again. Something about Davey's haggard face made him hesitate to ask any questions about that. "Why wasn't I chosen for this mission?" he asked at last.

"Because you were down for something else, is what I was told."

"The Eagle Squad?" Liam asked suddenly.

Davey nodded.

"But they aren't slated back for months yet. How long will this mission last, anyway?"

"Look around, you idiot. This is a death ship. No one is coming back."

Liam took a deep breath. He looked at the monitors, at the big old-fashioned ship that had obviously been pulled out of mothballs for one final run. He thought of the Captain who couldn't bear sending his unsuspecting crew into certain death.

"This is a joint operation, right? So how did they pick the crew?" he asked, his voice a rusty whisper.

Davey sighed. "Nearly every one of them has special skills. Some, like me, volunteered with eyes wide open, rather than face a long slow death from an incurable disease. A few are here instead of being court-martialed."

"And Boomer Kinkowsky? Why was he picked?"

"According to his record, the man is fearless. I gather he's apparently addicted to painkillers, but honestly, what does that matter here? It's a way for him to go out with honour. There are others in the group you could say the same thing about. Too much booze, pills, dope. Whatever. They hide it well, but eventually the weakness would win."

"God, what fools we were, trying to excel. All along they were looking for weaknesses?"

"You've landed in hell, boy. And there's nothing you can do about it."

"All we wanted was a chance to serve, to show what we could do."

"You've got that in spades," Davey said.

"That's why there are so many gays in this unit? Because they knew we'd welcome the chance to fight?"

"Who knows? You see the gold stars of the admiralty on my shoulder boards?"

"You do know the target, I take it?"

Davey snorted. "Always the cheeky one." He settled back and folded his hands across his stomach. "We're attacking the Al Forleze on Stasia Island. Headquarters of the Tronem Cult, which is secretly backed by the Ekvanistan Nations and used as a refuge for their terrorist leaders. Or so we were told."

"The Ekies! The bastards who drop bombs on our hospital bases in —"

"Right. This is the first move in Operation Hannibal."

"So who are we, the elephants?"

Davey shrugged. "More like mallards. We're the decoys. We take their minds off everything else back on the mainland while our second army moves into Ekvanistan through the mountains in a pincer movement to take the other three leaders of the Ekies. They've been getting in place for this for weeks."

"So that's where everyone was going."

"It'll bring them to their knees at last."

"No way they'll notice this dinosaur creeping up on them."

"Which is why we have ten supersonic Demon Deltas hidden on Deck B."

"So that's why we spent so much time training on the things. I should have guessed." And that's where Jack came in. Weapons expert, trained almost exclusively on Stealth Demons.

"Can you drive the damn things?" Davey asked.

"Yes."

"The idea is to bomb the hell out of them at low altitude, so you can't miss. After the first run, fly the loaded plane into the mountain." Davey shoved a pile of surveillance photos across the desk towards him, showing a mountain stronghold built into the side of the cliff.

There was silence as Liam looked them over. "So this really is a one-way ticket," he said.

"I told you, boy. You backed the wrong horse this time."

Silence stretched out between them for a few moments. The old ship strained and creaked through the storm, eating up the knots, going full throttle with no need to conserve fuel or engines.

Davey rolled his shoulders. He pulled a mickey out of his pocket and offered it to Liam, who shook his head. "We don't have a lot of hours left." He glanced at the wall of instruments and monitors. "The old tub is making pretty good time."

"The last briefing we had, the Ekie leaders were still in Algiers," Liam said. "That was two days ago. They've gone back?"

The Commander shrugged. "Probably misinformation. Our orders came in three days ago, straight from the top."

"Nothing since?"

"Nothing. At 1300 hours, they were still giving us the green light, in spite of this damned storm."

Liam stared at him across the desk as the ship pitched and yawed. That was the dark shadow in the man's eyes. Not the sickness that was slowly eating away at him, but the knowledge that his people were being sacrificed.

"Look, Davey, why do this? Why not hijack the planes and take off?"

"You're crazier than I thought." Davey started to laugh, then sputtered into a coughing fit. "And go where? Any idea how those things eat up fuel? Shit, isn't this why you enlisted? Why you volunteered for the elite Cobra unit? Why you did whatever you did to get on this damn tub when you weren't even chosen?"

Liam shook his head.

"Our orders are to wait, but you and I both know it's doubtful anyone will get back. Even if you do, this old tub will be blasted out of the water by their missiles as soon as they realize what's happening. We're not going home again, either."

"And who knows about this?"

"As far as our guys are concerned, senior bridge crew only. I don't know when you guys will be briefed. Soon, I imagine, orders direct to PDA."

"Shit. Bastards don't even have the guts to do it face to face." Liam watched the monitors, the images filling him with despair. Until one image flickered past. "Stop! Reverse! Get that image back!"

Davey flipped a switch and the landing deck came into focus. The Hawk copter from home base hung twisted and misshapen in the flashes of lightning, a twisted wreck, with Ramon's crushed body hanging from the cockpit.

"What the hell...."

"Sorry, Liam. We've only got a skeleton crew, and can't spare anyone to take away the body. It's tricky landing in heavy weather. Almost impossible to take off again. A sudden updraft must have slammed him against the ship's tower, snapping off the propeller."

Liam jumped up. "I've left a trail of bodies to get here," he said, "and I didn't do it to commit suicide. Where is Jack now?"

Davey brought up the ship's schedule on his monitor. "Deck B, checking gear. Look, I'm sorry you're here, but now you are there's nothing to be done. Go find your lover. You can die together in battle, which is, after all, what so many of us have fought for."

"But not as throwaways in a fake battle while the big boys do something more important!"

"You'll take out some of those terrorist types on Stasia, if that makes you feel any better."

"Yeah, sure. I'd feel better if I knew for a fact that Mr. Big and his cohorts were going to be there." Liam was staring at the image of the copter.

"It's no use," Davey said, his voice growing tired.

Liam headed for the door. "Give me the schemata of the ship. And the list of our wing crew."

"Knock yourself out." Davey threw him a small data sheet. "You now have less than one hour before scramble."

They could have sent several automatic drones loaded with bombs, Liam thought furiously as he made his way through the silent ship to Deck B. Why sacrifice people?

The answer came to him almost instantly. A drone couldn't handle the fancy flying this would demand, not at the speeds needed for surprise. Certainly not in this weather. And the Stasia force wouldn't expect a suicide attack from a big ship like this, even if they noticed them on their satellite feeds with the heavy cloud cover. Flying under the radar would catch them by surprise. The fool scheme might actually work.

JACK WAS TAKING a break with his group when Liam found them. He jumped up and ran over to Liam. "You made it after all! I knew you'd get here somehow!"

"I made it." Liam put an arm around Jack and drew him away from the others. "Look, what I'm going to tell you has to remain between us, understood?"

"What's the matter?"

"Swear!"

"Sure, love. I swear. What is it? You proposing again?" He laughed.

"Shut up and listen." As Liam told him what he had learned, he watched the colour drain from his lover's face.

"You trust Davey?"

"I do. We've got to get out of here. Now! Come on. The copter's a wreck, but we can take one of the Demons and get to an island."

"With a load of bombs."

"Dump 'em over the ocean. The fuel will last longer that way."

"And they have landing strips on this friendly island?"

"Stop grinning like that! I'll risk it."

"The US Navy will come looking for us," Jack pointed out. "Face it, sweetie. No one will shelter two gay deserters. And that's what we'd be."

"Jack, we've got to try! Come on!" He tugged his lover out the door and started down the corridor. "At least we'll be alive."

Jack pulled away. "No."

"They've made fools of us, don't you understand?"

"No, love. I'm where I want to be. Where I've dreamed of being since I was a kid."

"Jack, we don't have time for this." As if to back him up, the battle stations alert played out loud and clear from the ship's loudspeakers.

"I can't leave my crew," Jack said.

"Oh, for God's sake, it's a fucking suicide mission we weren't even told about. There's no oath of loyalty that covers that."

"I will not be the first gay officer to desert his post."

"Don't I mean more to you than some abstract principle?"

"I volunteered."

"For service in a special unit, yes. Not a secret suicide mission. Look who they've chosen, Jackie. Doesn't it strike you as odd that out of a group of twenty-eight, there are thirteen gays? Isn't that just a tad suspicious?"

"They picked the best people for the job. Like usual."

"Look. We're not the brave, the proud, the few. We're the halt, the lame, the gay."

"It doesn't matter!"

"It does! It's like ethnic cleansing! They're using us and throwing us away. Is this the new army you always dreamed about?"

"It's the one I'm in," Jack said stubbornly.

"Christ almighty! I'm trying to save you, you fucking idiot!"

"Liam, dearest, I'm a Marine. This is what I've wanted all my life. Only recently has it been possible. And now you're trying to take it away from me?"

"I want us to be together!"

"We are. We're the chosen."

"I wasn't! I followed you!"

"You *what*?"

"I took Boomer's place so I could be with you."

"Well, here you are," Jack said, shaking his head, a sad smile on his face. "You impetuous fool, you." He took out his PDA and checked the orders that flashed across the screen, then slipped it back inside his tunic. "I love you." He leaned close and kissed him tenderly. "*Semper fi.*" Then he turned away and started towards the door.

"Jack!" Liam's shout echoed eerily along the deserted corridor.

His lover paused, half turned, and looked back, his athletic body outlined against the driving rain hitting the deck outside. He held out a hand.

Liam walked towards him and took hold of his hand and held on tight as they walked together onto the deck, where the first of the Demons rose from the deck below into the swirling grey storm, like some futuristic ghost.

...the darkest evening of the year...

Candas Jane Dorsey

ALL NIGHT I struggled in dreams: hostages were taken, voyages, risks. All seemed to involve a lot of stairs, twisty, more up than down, dangerous, stone or carpeted, worn into hammocky slickness: when I awoke, I felt more tired than ever. The three upstairs were in it, and in the end the stairs went down into dark and cold.

When I awoke, though it was almost eleven, the day had hardly dawned, so grey and cloudy it was from the ice fog. The falling ice crystals were so meagre they could hardly be called snow. It was cold and flat and steely even at twenty-five to noon, when I went out to help Marilyn with the cars.

Marilyn and her partners drove cab to pay the rent on the upper two floors of the house where I lived in the main floor apartment. They didn't know that the landlord for whom the management company kept it was me, so we had become friends of a sort: I made no comment when they complained, on principle, about the landlord (*property is theft*), and they made no comment when I didn't. The cars had not been plugged in long enough and wouldn't start without a boost from mine, which so far always started without me having to use its block heater. We got the three cabs going after about twenty minutes in the snow, so I invited them down for a New Year hot chocolate while the cars' engines warmed.

Marilyn was grateful and relaxed, but Antoine and Adele

were, as always, a little uncomfortable and truculent. As I'd slept with them all, separately and together, at midsummer, it was an individual, not a situational, reaction. I poured the milk in mugs and put the mugs in the microwave, then stirred in cocoa and sugar. I watched the steam rise and shift in the draft from the inner room, as did they.

When are you doing the New Year? Adele said abruptly, for small talk.

Tonight, I said. That marked me as a traditionalist: since the calendar had been redeclared, New Year was celebrated on television at a new and more convenient time, but I was still measuring by the moon and the sun.

Us too, she said, and Antoine repressed his hushing gesture.

It's all right, I won't tell, I said. Do you want to do it together?

Marilyn smiled, Antoine scowled, Adele looked alarmed, but it was she who glanced at the others and then said, Sure, whatever.

Come at eleven, then, and we'll have our meal first.

They nodded and left.

I HAD SPENT the week getting ready. Some of the things I wanted to do were a bit different, and ingredients were hard to find. I had to go to a First Nations friend for wild rice for the stuffing, and promise some of my special soap to Xavier in the health food store before he took me in the back and sneaked some slivered almonds from his covert storeroom into my bag. In the fall I had dried my own cranberries after soaking them in orange juice, so I brought them up from the cold room and mixed them with Amanda's raisins and currants.

The wild rice was cooking already, mixed with some scented far-eastern red rice to make it stretch, and perhaps it was that sweet musky scent that had subliminally tipped the balance between yes and no for the wary upstairs threesome. Anyway, they promised attendance and left for their long shifts of driving, three badly-tuned engines generating steamy clouds of exhaust into the frozen grey air, three gypsy cabs with nothing but a telephone number on the paint-peeling doors to distinguish them from the ancient beaters driven by labourers and plumbers to midwinter job sites.

After I'd stuffed the meat's cavities with a dressing of wild rice, almonds, dried cranberries, and raisins, and placed the capacious roaster in my Aga's huge oven, I too went out again, armoured against the cold of the midwinter midday.

I felt the centre of the longest night stalking me, one heartbeat at a time. At one time my beats were sixty to the minute, but I'm fitter now so they've slowed, meaning that time is moving faster, more than a minute of subjective time for every sixty heartbeats, a quickening downhill pace.

I remember when my heart's minutes were eager, gentle, loving. Now, I fear that the winter solstice's fulcrum will not be sharp enough to lever me back to life. Like George Ansopo, dead these past three weeks, his books left to me, his clothing sent to charity and his furniture swarmed upon by his nieces and nephews, distant family who jetted in from across the continent to claim him dead as they never had while he was alive, I might decide, at that moment of maximum cold, to stop, not to return. George was one of my first beloved friends, and the last to leave me, though only the second to die. The children upstairs were diverting, but knew nothing of the shape my young heart took those three and a half decades ago.

* * *

As I DROVE through the erratically busy mid-day city, people, cars, and buildings seemed to appear and vanish into the dense ice fog as randomly as events and people had done in my life. In the same way I felt the car unpredictable at iced-over intersections, and once or twice it slid me through a stop sign or partway through a red light, missing collision only by random grace. Just so, I felt my life tilting out of balance, down a slippery rut, the career toward aphelion out of my control, and something disastrous and unavoidable waiting to strike me as I slid into its path.

I'd felt this way every midwinter, but worse for each of the last seven years, since Granita died. That solstice I thought would be the most heartbreaking, but in truth it passed before the numb shock wore off and I discovered that it is easier to weather a swift blow than it is to resist a slow decline. Heartbreak of that magnitude leaves a chasm open to erosion.

THE SHOP WAS cold, the back room almost enough for water to freeze in the pipes of the tiny washroom: I'd arrived just in time. The tenants who lived above and rented the shop next door, a jeweller, told me that the furnace had gone out about three o'clock the night before and they were still waiting for the gas company to come by. I had a look at the furnace and cleaned the nozzles and burners, but couldn't do much about the broken sensor.

I could, however, make trouble for the company, and as it was a holy day for us of the old religion, but a normal working day for the new believers, a repair "crew" – one stocky, irritable woman with chapped hands and a musty-smelling company jacket thick enough for polar expeditions – showed up within half an hour, telling us with annoyance that she had been on her way already. Whatever works.

While the restored-to-life furnace started to pour heat into the icy expanses of the shop and its mezzanine and the cavernous reaches of the storeroom, I put the small electric heater in the tiny toilet cubicle to stave off water-pipe disasters, then, still wearing my coat and the fingerless gloves I wear inside my mittens, began to sort, list, and shelve books from the boxes I had brought there the day before.

I felt as weak as the sun and the heat, as if the creeping cold would soon immobilize me. I knew the feeling would pass with the solstice – I had felt it every year for fifty-four years, but every year it crept further into my heart, and more than ever I wondered if this year the ritual would not do its rejuvenating work.

Is it the ritual, or just your imagination? the heretics say, now in control of the world, the present times washed with skepticism so that the touch of the Moon vanishes, the pull of the Sun is ridiculed, and I am, I am at odds with them all.

About 3:15 PM a customer came in shivering, and found the place tolerably warm, the furnace having blown heat without stopping for two and a half hours by then. She was a pallid-faced beauty with wide blue eyes and pale, almost snowy hair. I saw by what remained of its colour that it had once been vivid, Titian-bright perhaps, but that she had "gone white," as they say. She stood by the desk running her gloved fingers over the bindings of the books in the new boxes, and I realized I had seen her before, standing in the street outside George's shop yesterday while I packed the editions from the cabinets and from the barrister's bookshelf he kept behind the massive oak counter he affected in his draughty store.

Hello, I said. Are you looking for something from George's stock? Can I help you find a volume?

She smiled. I see you know who I am, she said.

No, madame, I simply recognize you from yesterday. I do not know you.

I am looking, she said, for a book I can use to guide me through various ... ceremonies of worship. I understand that you know something of the old ways. Perhaps you have such a manual or textbook?

I do not deal much in religious books, ma'am. I do have a small section of them in the back under the staircase there, mostly left over from the previous owner. And I do remember seeing a few in one of these boxes, but I haven't sorted the collection yet, and I bought it as a job lot. The previous owner, as you know, died recently.

Was he a friend? I'm sorry, she said offhandedly, and I smiled ferally at her, appreciating her wiles. Perhaps, she ventured – you see, I saw you at Books by George yesterday but I was afraid to come in....

I thought that this woman had rarely been afraid of anything, and told her so. My words wiped the simper from her face and she looked almost angry. Feel free to browse, I said. I've got quite a stack of work here, so I won't hover. Call me if you need me.

Thank you, she said, meaning something more basic, and moved briefly to the back corner by the stairs, then when she thought I wasn't looking, went out. But I saw her image reversed in the crackled, tarnished, crazed mirror behind the counter, and she glared at me as she left, and let the door slam, which put me on edge as none of her subterfuge had done. The Bureau puts an agent through my store about once every two months: she was a new one, and it was no accident she came at midwinter. I noticed with amusement, though, that she had been careful to make her visit before the early winter sunset, which was already bringing a false golden promise to the bare boulevard trees and making the downtown windows gleam and reflect more gold onto the shadowy canyons of street and avenue.

After she had left for the subway entrance across the street,

I went to the window and watched until the last of the golden glow was gone and the brilliant colourful sky had faded back into the grey and white and brown of the street. Then I returned to my task.

THE LAST BOX of George's books held the leather-bound specials, and I wiped each with a cloth to restore its oils before I placed it in my locked cabinet, joining the others that would never be sold. George had many small parchment editions, what are now called chapbooks, which he had made by hand, one after each midwinter for the past – I counted fifty-seven – years. Tonight we would celebrate the solstice, and then tomorrow I would begin such a book. George had left me more than his library.

At about six, the jeweller and her husband came in shyly, and found me with the last of the small editions in my hand and tears in my eyes, reading about last year. I blinked my vision clear, and put the book in my pocket. I met them halfway to the counter, and reached to shake his hand, then hers, but instead of gripping my fingers, she placed in them a small box. I looked at her, and she lowered her eyes.

A small gift Lan make for you, her husband said, his eyes also cast down. For today.

Because of the heat? I said, surprised. That's just my job, I don't need thanks.

Not the heat, whispered the jeweller. She wasn't confident speaking to others, as they had only been in the country for a couple of years. Most of her work was done for members of her own community, and I loved to hear the rapid rise and fall of their shadow voices faintly through the wall. Sometimes they would come into the bookstore, where I kept a small stock of foreign-language books near the door, and would browse until they found something, or bring their used books to sell or trade.

Not the heat, she repeated. For today. This day.

She was flushed and uneasy. I bent my gaze to the box, a beautiful, intricate paper construction that unfolded its wings when I pulled a small midnight-blue tab on the side. Inside, a small gold brooch in the shape of a sprig of evergreen, delicate gold needles, and a tiny prickly cone of seeds, so beautiful, and in red gold too, as if the fire were about to take it and germinate the seeds, offering new promise. It was very beautiful, and if they knew what it was, very dangerous.

I make today, she said. From tree outside (she pointed toward the side of the building where a couple of small pines grew among the tangle of willow and aspen filling the empty third of the lot) and tonight we burn broken piece.

They both bowed a little.

They knew. Shaken, I bowed back to them, and they smiled. Then we embraced formally, and they giggled a bit, and I laughed.

To the light, I said formally.

To the light? she repeated tentatively.

Yes, I said. That is what we say. Here. And you reply, light to you.

Also we say, she said, and repeated it in her language, with me clumsily trying the imitation. Clumsy, but it pleased them, and we bowed again.

I have roast beast, I said impulsively, and an altar. Come ye at one hour to midnight, you can share the feast.

We are honoured, but we have large family, many friends come to eat, we go now to place, said Kemao, gesturing vaguely eastward.

Lan nodded, smiling downward into her clever, creative

hands, which were folded together at her solar plexus, small mittened hands pressed together as if in secret delight. Thank you, she whispered.

The thanks is all mine, for this wonderful gift, I said reverently, touching the pine-cone gently, and Lan smiled even more, shot a glance sideways at me as we all bowed again and they turned to go.

As they left the shop, I saw with surprise that as I had unpacked George's books, my concentration focused, the snow had begun to blow, hurling itself viciously against the bay windows.

They had already locked their home and shop doors, but Kemao darted back to rattle the grille just in case, then they walked away across the street, moving against the wind with difficulty, and vanished into the cold furious eddy above the subway entrance, a whirlwind made orange and granular and acrobatic by the diffracted, diffused glow of the streetlights.

I stood inside the shop door for a long time after I had turned the deadbolt, watching the blizzard into which they had disappeared, holding the box. Then I took the pin out and held it in my hand even longer, its gold warm against my palm and its needles gently prickling my skin in an effect miniature to the real thing waiting for me at home. Finally I pinned it to my shirt-front between the top button and the decorative stitching on the placket above the rest of the buttons, and turned to go back to the counter, the box still unfolded in my hand.

When I reached the counter, I set the box down and attempted to reclose it, but when I pressed it into its previous shape, it gave a little pop like a pine knot popping in a fire very far away, and exploded out of my hands into a flat sheet unscored by any fold lines. The sheet floated down to the counter, where it began to curl at the edges, and then burst into a brief hot white flame, after which there was nothing but a small damp scorch on the counter and a tiny drift of silver ash.

The old ways were not dead, at least in this small building. I touched my finger to the ash, then to my tongue, a taste of pitch and perhaps magnesium and, overlaying all, some eastern spice, cardamom perhaps? Something dusky and generous.

It was time to close the store and go home. The beast would be cooked, the house dark and cool, and I had a lot to do before the solstice. A lot to do even before my guests arrived, for that matter. I left by the back door, checking the furnace and turning off the heater under the water pipes on the way.

EVEN MY SWEET little car was cranky, though it started up like a dream as always. As I drove along the river road, where the streetlights seemed to have been blown out by the wind, I was almost the only vehicle, my lights making the visibility zone into a capsule of mystery questing through a hostile, obscure unknown universe. Through twisted bare branches hung with hoar, the reflective street signs came into view long before the rest of their surround, then drifted past into the darkness I left behind.

When I reached the curved approach to the bridge and found those lights on, it was as if I had emerged from a wormhole. I crossed the bridge through heavy river fog, but up the hill on the other side I lifted out of the valley mist and onto a cold, crisp plain where the houses lining the curved streets were pods of secrecy, curtains drawn against cold and night.

My own house looked massy and clever, but light blazed from inside, so I could see the decorated tree, the stag-skull mounted above the mantel, and two of my neighbours moving in their upstairs kitchen.

I parked in the garage beside two tired gypsy cabs, rimed with street salt and grime and with chunks of snow falling behind their tires from tattered mudflaps. I noticed that Marilyn had thought to plug in the block heater, but Antoine had not: she must have arrived first, I thought, and I found an extension cord for his poor cold machine. Everyone warm at solstice, that's the rule. Or at least, the effort.

The savoury smell of roast meat met me as I unlocked and opened the outer back door. Marilyn called hello down the stairs, and I called back up to her as I unlocked my kitchen door.

To the light! she called down. Don't cook veg, I'm bringing some yam and sweet potato! One of my regular fares has a garden.

Light to you! Hey, that's great, I yelled, thinking, one less task for me.

And turnip and pumpkin, called Antoine. I cook like my father did, with butter. *Merde*, I mean, to the light.

I laughed. Light to you! *Merci!* I went in, wondering if that would give me more time to suitably prepare my spirit.

I pulled off my gear and shook the snow off my coat, then walked into the bedroom to change into a long warm robe, pinning it shut over my heart with Lan's gold pine-sprig. Back in the kitchen, I reached for the mitts and pulled the beast-pan from the oven. When I took off the roaster's lid, the roast's flesh was pleasantly crusty and so well done it almost fell from the bone, and the wild rice had swelled, bursting open the cavities in which it had been stuffed. My mouth watered. I carved the meat in the pan, thinking of the New Year as it would be for the majority, the new believers, twelve days from now, with their twelve meatless dishes, one for each new-calendar month, and their stingy bird in the evening of the next day, twelve bites each by electric light.

That reminded me to light the candles around the house, and so when the platter was in the warming oven, I went about placing floating candles into antique glass bowls, glasses, and long dripless ones into candelabra, lighting them all with the little propane igniter. Then around again, closing shutters and pulling drapes, until the night was concealed and the rich golden light amplified.

I have nothing against night by itself. In fact, I may love it more than day, its long view to infinity instead of day's arrogant limitations. There have been many clear solstice nights, warm or cold, when I have gone up to the roof walk and lain across the tiles, watching the winter stars whirl, The Hunter in all his arrogant beauty, his trailing hounds howling at midnight, the shrinking Virgins huddling together against his inevitable virility, the noble Old Queen surveying all, the Firedrake spreading its prophetic wings, and all the rest of the crew. I knew them all. If this night had not been a maelstrom of cold and snow, I'd have gone up there to say goodbye to George, perhaps seen if he sat with the Old Queen, or hunted virgins (if so, I smiled, they had better be boys, for he never had the slightest interest in the other kind), or simply lolled on the horizon and basked in the Dragon's fire. But the midwinter night was murderous, and I did not want that vengeful storm to see our warm ritual, any more than I wanted the Bureau's cold agents who no doubt lurked somewhere in the chilly shadows.

Once the windows were curtained, I took my little electronic box and swept the rooms for eavesdroppers, finding one tiny knob of a microphone, which I moved to the cellar, hiding it under the burners of the furnace, where it would hear nothing but the roar of fire and fan, and eventually would fail from the heat. I could have crushed it, but this would be more satisfying, for it would keep the Ice Queen and her henchfolk in some cramped cold van, monitoring sounds just past the verge of audibility, until the cold night was over. I was not usually that vindictive, but I missed George, the trio above were yet too young and slight to trust with my heart, and it was a nasty night altogether. I touched the brooch, however, and felt my spirits lift. Next year perhaps I would be able to join Kemao and Lan and their community,

perhaps bring a small boring family instead of a lonely boring self
– hope springs eternal, I thought, but caught myself with a snort:
wasn't that what this night was about?

I HEARD ADELE kick her way through the back door, swearing and
stomping snow from her feet.

To the light! I called. Did you plug in your cab?

Sod it! she shouted, and slammed the door behind her as
she went. She returned more temperate in a couple of minutes.
Light to you, I mean. Thanks.

I handed her a cup of warm apple cider with cinnamon. Warm
up, I said, then take some to Em and Ah upstairs. She grinned at
the use of the pet names, handed back the empty mug and un-
wound herself from her layers of tatterdemalion winter gear.

She saw me watching her hang up sweaters, scarves, and
coats, and blushed. Sodding heater doesn't work much, she muttered. I send what there is back to the passenger seat.

I'll have a look at it tomorrow, if we can get a heater going
in the garage, I said.

Oh, you don't have to…. She trailed off as I went back to
the stove and ladled out a mug each for the two above, refilled
hers, and left her with the challenge of getting them upstairs.

I don't have to, I thought, but it was the only way to make
contact. If I only had the energy I used to have, I thought; if only
the turning of the year promised more than a greeting-card hope
and a long uphill climb: yet now, more than ever before, I instead dreaded that obliterating solstice moment, that possibility
of overthrown weakness, that window into a darkness that had no
stars, had no smooth dark skin, only entropy and oblivion. Both
of my beloved had died as the darkness grew: close to the point
of midwinter, flagging and failing despite their determination to

go on to the light. The newspapers were fuller than usual with death notices at this time of year: old people who could not fight through to another spring, sick people who lost heart, heart failure they call it, or were eaten by their cancers or obliterated by strokes and aneurisms.

I would not have it; I would not be one of them: but I would be one of them some day, and this creeping knowledge disheartened me. What humankind always fears: negation. I was no longer special. I had rubbed down with age into any declining animal, a creature of fear, loss, and grief, hoping against all knowledge for vigour and immortality. Immortality the old religion had never offered, and indeed, were we to have sins in our faith as the new believers did, it would be a sin to embrace such a wish, a dream against nature: stasis.

I would lead the ritual tonight, but unless this heartsickness eased, my leadership would be hollow, sacrilege. The three above clattered down the stairs and suddenly the kitchen was bustling, Marilyn and Antoine putting casserole dishes into the warming oven, Adele pouring me a mug of cider, flashing colours and youthful bustle. I am only fifty-four, I thought; why do I feel so foolishly old?

I looked at the three who would share meat with me tonight. Marilyn's round dark face was shadowed by her hair as she bent over the open oven door. She wore red as she often did, and her skin looked rich and luscious against its brilliance. In her brief time upstairs, Adele had changed into a velvet skirt and a low-cut embroidered blouse, its lace low on her triceps to show off her lucent skin and lovely shoulders and breasts. Antoine's thin bony face was flushed, his dark eyes glittering in the candlelight, and he wore a loosely woven shirt through which his slim, muscled torso showed provocatively. If one of them would understand something, anything, would reach out to me, this night would be very different.

We finished our preparations surprisingly quickly, for four people who had never performed such a cooking ritual before, and it was just after ten when we were ready to eat.

Just a moment, I said, and went to the living room. Pulling a footstool over to the fireplace, I climbed up and reached for the deer skull. My mother had found it on one of the coastal islands, deep in the humus, clean and white, unbroken by shot or arrow. It was from one of the tiny deer who live only on those islands, and I imagined a tiny perfect stag, reaching the end of his dignified life, lying gracefully down at the foot of a cedar and consigning his magical life force back to the Universe. Not that I necessarily believed in that magic any more, I thought sourly, but still, at the memory of my mother and her gift of the skull to me, one midsummer when Granita and George had been young, and happy together, Mother still alive, Father still aware, and the power still strong in all of us, tears stung my eyes, and my hands tightened on the bone until it felt warm in my grip. I thought I heard a noise behind me, but when I turned, no one was there.

I returned to the dining room, where Marilyn was placing the last of the platters on the table, and nestled the stag's skull on the centrepiece of pine boughs. Antoine sighed, and Adele nodded.

My father always did that, she said.

I am no one's father, I said sharply. Granita had died of complications of an ectopic pregnancy, though these people couldn't know that.

I know, Adele said, and blushed, and turned away to sit down.

We served each other, as was the custom, and then we stood to say the words. *To the light, and light to us …* and onward: they knew it as well as did I, and despite my resolve to be safe I felt a surge of tenderness for them.

Where did you get this meat? Antoine asked. Since the new

government regulations, strong red meat had been scarce, so I'm sure he voiced only what the rest of them thought, yet Marilyn glanced at him in shock.

It was George's, I said. He gave it to me before he died. I thought it was a good idea to do my best by it, since it's probably what caused the death of him who would have been eating it with us today if he could have.

Adele laughed suddenly. Better eat up then, she said, and lifted a silver fork to stab another juicy morsel. She held it aloft: To George, who knew what we would want.

We repeated her gesture, and To George! we all toasted. I thought of my good friend gone, my lover so many years, then my colleague and friend after he found loving too foolish and dangerous, and I bit angrily down on the piece of crackling I'd chosen to toast him with, savage with loss and grief.

A savage cannot lead anyone to the light, even himself. A deep and desperate sadness welled up again.

To George, I thought, who still was willing to risk prison by taking a bow out into the silent woods to hunt our Horned King, to say the words, to borrow the god's life for our rituals. Whose heart gave out as he dragged the carcass back to the road, and who barely made it to town before he collapsed. In hospital, he called for me as his next of kin, told me where to go to find the stag, gave me his bookstore key, and died. Now we ate his meat in honour of the Queen who would release the sun into our custody, but my thoughts stayed in the darkness.

I wished suddenly for some other kind of religion, where the sharing of meat and drink, instead of joyous, was some kind of sanitized cannibalism, where this meal would have been consecrated to a darker, angrier god. Impulsively, I said so to the others.

It would have to be an unhappy god, said Antoine. One born of unhappiness. What would be the opposite of our Lady and her Love, and their Child of Light?

Perhaps the child of rape, said Adele darkly, a story waiting to be told there, I felt sure.

Of a virgin, said Marilyn, oblivious to Adele's flushed cheeks. A virgin unwilling, or talked into it by some agent of the rapist. (She snorted.) You know, *you'll like it, really you will....* So she says, well, that's the last time I date a god if *that's* what it's like....

A god angry and judgmental, said Antoine, who wants to punish ...

We all fell silent.

... sin, I finally finished his sentence. A New Belief, perhaps, that sin is in everyone because the god has sinned?

We looked at each other, appalled. Finally: I never thought of it that way before, said Adele in a small voice, and Antoine said, we were just making a joke, dear little Adele; his voice quivered a little however, and none of us, especially not Adele, believed him. Surrounded by the new believers, in our enclosed sphere of golden candlelight, we shivered as bleak midwinter crept into our bones.

I'm sorry, I said. I didn't mean to lead us into *that* dark corner! and for some reason, that, rather than our shared "joke," was what made us all laugh until we were out of breath, laugh because it was so ridiculous, laugh because we had to.

To the light, I said, finally, which set us off again.

Light to you, said Adele finally. Shall we clear away the plates? There is only a short time left until the moment.

How do you know? I asked.

Can you not feel it? she said. Eating your entrails as we ate this stag's heart?

Yes, I said, but I do not know many others who can.

You know me, she said. You know us. We all can. It's why we're here.

Simple words enough, but humbling to me, as I had spent

all day thinking perhaps I was some outmoded avatar of a forgotten life force, alone among new believers in sin and old believers by habit only. I stood to ready myself for the ritual.

I will call you in on the moment the light decides to return, I said formally, but Adele was young.

We'll stack the dishes and get the berries and the cup ready, she said.

I sighed. The berries are in the pantry, I said. I thawed them yesterday.

All right.

I held the kitchen door open so she could enter with the stack of my good plates, my grandmother's silverware atop the meal's scraps. I imagined they'd be saving those for their cat. Mine had died last spring, and I hadn't gotten another. Maybe I would next spring, I thought, and as I did I heard Marilyn saying to Antoine, I tell you, he was *crying!* and Antoine saying, what does he have to cry for?

Adele met my eyes. I'll tell them, she murmured.

Tell them what? I said, just as low.

That you have two decades more to cry for than we do, and secrets we will never know.

I let the door go and watched it swing to behind her. Then, taking the old deer skull, I went into the inner room, which was still dark but for the tiny flame on the altar. I placed the skull carefully beside the embroidered circle of linen where the chalice would rest, and raised my gaze to the invisible sky, admitted to the room by a lofty skylight, which on a milder night I would have opened.

Mother, I said, *be with me*. I meant our queen.

Father, I said, *be with me*. I meant our king.

Exiting the ritual for a moment, I pressed my hands to my heart, and felt the prickle of Lan's gold pine sprig. The feeling sent a wave of warmth through my breast, though for an unheroic second I thought it was going to be angina, so weak I had become.

The universe helps those who help themselves, my father used to say, but my mother had had other thoughts, and she had said to me once, we are like cells in a body, and the body, though it is infinite, depends on our finite and delicate services to sustain its immortality. A cell must be fed. There is no shame in asking for what we need to do our work.

I am tired and faint of heart, I said to the rest of the vast organism of which I was such a meagre part, and death has stopped being my friend. I don't want to take risks in love, and I don't want to give away any more of my life to these careless children who don't even remember to plug in their cars. Universe, give me the strength I need to live for the rest of my life.

The moment of death was upon me, the longest moment of the longest night, the instant that is an eternity of risk for the children of woman and man, and as it gripped my heart I heard from the open door of the sanctuary three sighs that blended with mine in a harmony as ancient as the sun and moon, as the tilted planet, as ancient as each young being upon the earth. My heart –

– kept beating. I reached the tip of my finger to the tiny flame, and it leapt to me, and grew. I gave the call –

Come in, ye children of light. The light still lives!

– and in came the three, Adele carrying the chalice, Antoine the fruit, and Marilyn the pine boughs. The light that tipped my fingers grew, and I threw it toward the candles so that my hands would be ready to receive our lady's peace. The room blazed suddenly with the fire of life.

The chalice was cool in my hands, but when I sipped, the mead was hot. I leaned my mouth to Adele, smiling without swallowing, then giving her the kiss of mead, and she swallowed the honey wine slowly.

To Antoine, I nodded and gave the second kiss of mead, and as he swallowed it he placed a handful of berries into my mouth, saskatoons from the height of summer, picked in the river valley under the noses of the Bureau, at perihelion, and raspberries from my own garden, a mixture of bitter and sweet, like our existence. I turned to Marilyn, and saw him reach to Adele, her mouth open to the berries.

I couldn't help it: it is Marilyn I love best, I thought, and I smiled more widely, then bent my head again to the cup. Mead into her mouth and she swallowed, Antoine gave her the berries, and finally, as she held evergreen above my head, I could take my own healing draught and swallow berries and honey wine.

I turned and poured the libation onto the tiny brazier flame, which flared up in our faces. Adele laughed; Antoine made a sound in his throat, a precursor to later pleasures. Marilyn reached across the altar with the branches in her left hand and I saw the pale flash of her palm as she placed them on the renewed fire.

The rest of the ritual – the words, the songs, the kisses and embraces – was performed in that sparkling, cracking fire, smelling of new forests and burnt honey.

At its conclusion, after the traditions are carried out, there is only choice: how each will pledge their renewal is a personal one. Should they choose not to stay, I would light the pine log fire in the living room myself, and in that yule light I would begin this year's book. Should they choose me, I would try not to run away.

It was Adele who was wise, Antoine who was daring, but Marilyn who held my heart then in her pitch-smeared fingers. And it was she who reached for my heart, found the catch of Lan's gold pin and released it, she who brushed my robe back over my shoulders. Then they all came to me laughing, and pulled me down onto the fur rug, and brought honey to me, and me to them, each in our own way.

The brazier burned low, the candles too. Through the sky-light, I saw that the wild wind had blown away the cloud, and instead of a white and ochre obscurity, I saw the stars. South it was, the Hunter's path, the Virgins' home, and if they meet, the joy of it will obliterate the universe.

As did, for an eternal moment, the blaze of brilliant happiness with which these lovers brought me out of the darkness, though as I lay back and flung my arms wide to receive it, one finger caught the pin on Lan's brooch, and I brought blood to the climax after all. After the universe began to reassemble itself and the others close around me for warmth and rest, I sucked a drop of the blood's cuprous sweetness from my finger, and got with it remnants of the meal and of the juices of these three intruders into my heart.

Dozing, I found myself in an ocean of random thoughts: shivering memories of recent touch, and the old loves new touch cannot help recall: the first, the most present, the unsuspecting last, and the mixture was potent with lust, fear, contentment, fury. I feared death, I loved them, I loved: aging limbs, ancient past, dangerous future, careless youth, gypsy cabs, books, sex. One of the candles popped, then went out.

Let's do this more often, Marilyn said.

You are a sweet man, said Antoine, and I would.

I … I started, hesitating, not knowing what to say.

Tell a secret, interrupted Adele, then burrowed her head down in embarrassment – but it was the rest of us who should have been embarrassed, forgetting the last thing.

I know … I spoke slowly, afraid … all of you. Better than I wanted to, but less than I will. I am afraid, but I promise to try not to let that stop me.

I know you cried tonight, said Marilyn. I will reach for you from time to time, in case you need help.

I know you own this house, said Adele. I'll quit complaining about the plumbing.

I know you own Marilyn, said Antoine. I'll try not to mind too much.

No, said Marilyn. *I* own Sasha.

I noticed she promised no mercy on that account. I licked the taste of meat, blood, honey, and come from my lips, thinking that tomorrow I had a book to begin, and was silent until Antoine prodded me, said, tell me, you beast.

I was on my own: I own nothing and no one, I said – at which they all laughed, too knowingly by far – and on that new-year's lie we went to sleep, creatures together in the long, passing dark, who had hoped for light, and found it.

FROM Homogenous TO Honey

SCRIPT- NEIL GAIMAN
PENCILS- BRYAN TALBOT
INKS - MARK BUCKINGHAM
LETTERS- STEVE CRADDOCK

GOOD EVENING AND WELCOME TO OUR NEW UNIVERSE.

AS YOU CAN TELL, WE'VE MADE A NUMBER OF IMPROVEMENTS ON THE OLD ONE.

TODAY WE'RE GOING TO LOOK AT HOW OUR PRESENT UTOPIA WAS ACHIEVED.

LIGHTS, PLEASE!

THE REMOVAL OF A CONCEPT FROM SOCIETY IS ALWAYS FRAUGHT WITH POTENTIAL PROBLEMS.

WHERE DO WE START?

FIRST SLIDE, PLEASE.

I THINK WE CAN ALL SEE THE PROBLEMS HERE, HMM?

NOT VERY UTOPIAN, IS IT?

THE OBVIOUS PLACE TO START WAS WITH BOOKS, REPOSITORIES OF IDEAS.

DANGEROUS.

EXAMINE, PLEASE, A BOOK WHICH PRESENTS A POSITIVE IMAGE OF INVERSION.

A BOY'S OWN STORY
EDMUND WHITE

THAT WAS EASY.

WHAT THEN TO DO ABOUT SOMETHING THAT CONTAINS A FAIRLY SYMPATHETIC CATAMITE?

My Long Ago Sophia

Diana Churchill

I WAS AT MY son Blake's apartment when I got a call from my annoying old friend Jackie, who was determined to keep in touch with me. Her voice sounded the same as it always had – forceful and lascivious towards me, even though we're both in our sixties now. On the tiny screen embedded in the back of my wrist, her grey hair and no makeup made her face look like a moving pencil sketch below the date: 28/12/2026.

"Lauren, did you hear? About Sophia's son?" she asked. My wrist and hand stiffened as I answered that I hadn't.

"He's dead. It's all over the news." I knew Jackie was expecting me to react with shock or at least morbid curiosity, but what I felt was my own regret – private and long locked away.

"He blew the whole place up. Some sort of human reproduction lab, crazy bugger. Must run in the family, remember –"

"Not now, Jackie." *Don't be a bitch.* My memories of Sophia were personal, isolated, and devastating to me.

As if reading my mind, she added, "I don't mean to sound bitchy but, ya' know, Sophia was so fuckin' screwed with him, 'course he would blow like his father did."

"I've got to go," I said at last, then I shut her face off on my wrist without another word, though. I didn't mean to be rude.

Rude.

I sat on my son's couch. *Sixty-three years old and still trying not to be rude – even to people who're that way to me.* I should be used to Jackie by now; her comments about Sophia had always been cruel. I closed my eyes and pressed my forehead against the heels of my hands, picturing Sophia as I had known her all those years ago. Her image came to me as vividly as always – not just from the picture I kept programmed in the chip in my wrist, but from the images I kept in my mind. In my favourite picture of her, she is wearing shorts and a plunging peasant top, its strings dangling across her breasts. Her hair is brown, nothing special, but she wears it loose and wild, even keeping the few strands of grey woven through it. I can still see her; I haven't been able to hear her voice, though, since she'd died.

Another phone call from Jackie, over twenty years ago, made sure of that.

JACKIE HAD BEEN the one to find Sophia dead, and to describe the scene to me. She had detailed how Sophia's legs were hanging off the edge of the bed, as if she'd been trying to get up, and how the bottle of sleeping pills had been thrown into the hall. I've dreamt of the scene a million times: her wild hair spread out over the pillow, her lips breathlessly apart. Sometimes I kiss her and her eyes spring open, and she lurches up to strangle me. After describing her death, Jackie then read the suicide letter that Sophia had left addressed to me. Her words were angry, pleading, hopeful – and in the end, broken. All of her desperate devotion spilled out over the phone to me, but in Jackie's churlish voice, destroying forever my lover's true voice in my head.

* * *

I LIFTED MY head, opened my eyes, and looked around, as if to confirm that I was still sitting on my son's couch. I raised my wrist close to my mouth and whispered, "Images," then, "Farmhouse," and waited until a tiny picture came up on my communicator's screen. The image was of five women in front of the farmhouse where we'd all lived. I sat in the middle, Sophia and Jackie on either side of me. The details of us were too small to make out, but I knew them by heart: Sophia's leg was over mine, her arm wrapped around me, and I was looking at her. I'd come to the farm with three young children and a husband who at first begged me to come back because he loved me, and then threatened to rip out my throat if I didn't. Sophia had torn into him on my behalf, although it was Jackie who'd actually scared him away.

The picture on my wrist was so small and remote I had to raise my wrist right in front of my eyes to make it out, like the ancient slides my grandmother used to bring out. I wanted enlarge my images. I lay my wrist on the controls embedded in the arm of the couch and the screen on the wall sprang to life, asking me to speak my selections clearly. My voice sounded strange in the stark, quiet apartment.

Lonely.

"Farmhouse – two-thousand and two to two-thousand and five – scroll all at five seconds," I said. A minute later I said, "Freeze." And there we were – our picture on the wall, life-size. All five of us, arms around each other and legs intertwined. If only we hadn't posed in front of that damn dilapidated porch, with the fretwork dangling like arms from a monster. The next picture was of Sophia's tall son Joel and my three kids, so young, running barefoot even though the leaves had already fallen. We had no idea what was to happen to us. Giddy, blissful, romantic. Three years my children and I had lived like that.

Living openly and in love with Sophia on the farm was the opposite of everything I had ever known. I'd been brought up

Christian — the born-again kind. At fifteen I'd met my husband at the *God's Little Soldiers* summer camp. We were both graduates and counsellors there. There were moments of peace for me at that camp — my parents were pleased I was dating a church boy. I remember loving the children's faces as they sang, but I could never remember loving the boy. However, he fit the Lord's and my parents' plan for me, and we courted and petted and waited until we were married before screwing. Waiting for him had been easy for me. "She's a good girl!" Preacher Baxter would say. *No, I'm not*, I would think. At night, faceless females caressed my body in dreams that confused and tormented me. I wanted to be that good girl everyone wanted — at the time it seemed the only route — so as a teen I never fought to break out of my born-again cocoon, one of many regrets in my life.

Most of the pictures that followed were of Blake and my other two, Owen and Chelsea, as kids. There was Chelsea, sitting on the kitchen floor, banging a lid against a pot — a time-immortal toddler shot. The next one was of the three of them playing outside on a beautiful day, shining like child ghosts in my adult son's living room. Then a close-up of Sophia's face, its size overwhelming, almost menacing to me. I snapped, "Shut off," to the wall and it cut away to dark and then the lights came back on, returning me to Blake's sterile apartment.

I glanced around to ground myself. The couch and chairs were cold leather, with stiff pillows that did nothing to ease their rigidity. The floor was blond maple, with detail so random, according to Blake, that no one could tell it was fake. *I can by the way it feels on the soles of my feet.* In the corner was a stainless steel door leading to his six-foot-square virtual reality room. It was "expensive, new, cutting edge," he had bragged, and as close to time travel as my generation would get. He hadn't said so, but I knew I wasn't to touch it. A rich uptight bachelor, my Blake was, with a stainless steel closet instead of a family as his pride. I pushed his expensive pillows off the couch, stared at them on the floor, and then picked them back up. It was my fault he'd turned out this way. We could have stayed on the farm instead.

I had been curious about the stainless steel door in his living room on the very first day of my arrival. The door had slid open automatically for us, as if the room had a mind of its own. Gloves were wired to a leather reclining chair that spun in place to face any wall. Blake smoothed the gloves down on the arms of the chair, his silent signal for me to not pick them up. Dangling from the ceiling at the end of a flexible tube was a helmet that looked so large I imagined it swallowing my head. "Most of the V.R. cafés use this system," he had said, adding that he had top-of-the-line accessories so he could fully experience virtual reality with all his senses. I refrained from asking the obvious – did he use it for sex? Instead I asked if it could re-create a person's voice, and he explained how he could scan in vocal sounds. I thought of Sophia while he was talking. Would she feel real, with a voice? Could a wired-up closet really make me forget that my soul mate was dead?

THE NEWS ABOUT Joel made me feel Sophia's suicide as freshly as when it first happened. I remained silent in my son's living room, not wanting to turn on anything from outside this sequestered space. Joel's death would be a feature story. He'd grown into a cult leader with a global audience, having leveraged his infamous family name and using the power of virtual reality in his broadcasts to brainwash his following. I had listened to him once, out of curiosity, and quickly turned him off in disgust. Joel had been raging against technology which replaced a mother's womb, claiming this spelled doom for humanity. He was the kind of person who never spoke directly against women's rights, carefully choosing phrases like "moral choice" instead. As usual, I thought, there was some truth in what Jackie had said: Sophia had poisoned him.

WHAT HAD SHE done to me? Sophia would repeatedly ask me it had been hard to give up my family and my religion for her – a point of pride, I think.

"As long as I have my kids," I'd always reply. But I could never get her to speak about her own family, even to say much about Joel, who was living with us at the time. Her father was a descendent of the Jim Jones cult, so I figured her mother was a safer topic.

"Was your mother beautiful?"

"Pretty. Not beautiful, like you."

"You're just in love with me."

"It's not a sin to admit you're beautiful." She would stroke my hair and kiss my cheek with a tenderness that no one else ever had. She would always twist our conversation back to me, and I'd always allow her to do it, so I never did get her to talk. Maybe if I'd tried harder, instead of succumbing to my vanity, I might have saved her. That thought has haunted me.

Regret.

The trigger that led to her death came in August of 2004, when I told Sophia that I intended to send my kids to public school. We argued about it a lot: Joel was home-schooled and look at how he turned out – his being so smart has nothing to do with the pitiful job you've done with him – the fuckin' professionals will butt in 'cause we're gay – in this day and age? – the Children's Aid already came after me once 'cause of it – that's just your lame excuse for neglecting your son ... I had been so sure, so stupidly, stupidly sure. I accused her of being lazy with

Joel and of abusing drugs. I told her he'd confided in me, not in her, that he was taking his high school equivalency exams.

"He wants to get the hell away from you and I'm encouraging him to do it!"

It took us longer than usual to make up after that, but as always, we did. We smoked joints in bed, laughing and drawing lines over our naked bodies with the kids' magic markers. Blake, who must have been about eight at the time, walked in on us just as I was scribbling my name on Sophia's butt. Hysterical, we thought, and we laughed and laughed and I let Sophia love me again, instead of chasing after him to talk.

The first call came in the winter. "My name's Bruce Lighthorn," he said. "I'm a worker with Children's Aid." He had a solicitous, disingenuous manner, suggesting I take my time getting a pen and did I have a calendar handy? He wanted to set up a convenient time to visit.

"Of course," I answered. "May I ask what for?"

His reasons were vague and hard for me to follow. I couldn't concentrate. Something was strange about a story one of my children had written. The teacher had reported it to them. Which teacher? Which child? I couldn't follow. He didn't want to get into it over the phone, he said. I hung up abruptly, panic washing down from my neck to my bowels. Sophia would strangle me.

The first meeting was cordial, even pleasant. Bruce Lighthorn was young and he took lots of notes. "Kids will be kids," he'd said, smiling and nodding as I talked. But he kept asking me about drugs, about why so many adults lived in the house, and then, jokingly, what we had against men. Then he asked how the kids felt about their father.

"Was he the one who called you?" I asked, my voice getting tight.

"No, as I've told you, it was their teacher, but we are obligated by law to contact him."

I remember standing there at the door, petrified, as the cheap-suited bastard walked out. Bruce's visit kept at me. My husband and his parents petitioned for custody. No one said a word about me being gay, but I knew I had to move out or they'd take my children away. At first Sophia was furious and defiant about this injustice, as if she couldn't believe her own warnings. But when she realized I wasn't going to let her fight for me – that I was determined to leave – she raged at me, then pleaded with me not to go, until I did – and then she simply crumpled.

"We'll still see each other," I'd promised her, and for a while we did, but she got stoned every time. She accused me of instigating the whole thing so I'd have an excuse to leave her. Or if I hadn't, that I was simply running again in fear.

"Either way," she said, "all I've done for you hasn't changed one thing. You're still the same pathetic spirit who allowed herself to be bred so young." I defended myself as having sacrificed a lot for my kids, something she might have tried with her son. She hurled herself toward me at that one, but stopped short of grabbing my neck. I could always get to her by bringing up her son.

A TIMER BUZZED in the kitchen, my son's way of reminding me to eat lunch. All I wanted was a cup of tea, if I could remember how he'd shown me to prepare it. I stared at the control panels on the kitchen cupboards, looking for an icon that suggested tea. *God forbid he should just leave something out on the counter for me.* I finally had to spell out my request, then a tea bag slid down the chute. *He lives out of a fucking vending machine!* I spent the next ten minutes trying to find a kettle before I remembered where the nozzle that dispensed boiling water was.

I stared at the now-blank wall where the farmhouse picture had been projected life-size. Her face was sanguine, her leg over mine, her hand on my hip; could I feel that again in my son's virtual reality closet?

My tea was ready. Blake would not be home from work for four more hours. I could go out, I supposed, but there was nowhere in this city that I knew. It would have been easy to tell his PC where I was, my interests and my age, so it could give me recommendations. I went to the window instead, but the view was so high it was useless, unless I was looking for a good place to jump.

The door to the virtual reality room opened as I walked past it on my way back to the couch. *You know you want to try,* I imagined it saying to me. I paused, set the teacup on the fake floor, and stepped in. The helmet dangled above my head; the chair spun around to face me. *Must he always have sex sitting up?* I sat in the chair and dared to put on the gloves, then reached and pulled the helmet down over my head. Sensors in the helmet detected I was there, and the walls started flashing dark and inquiring. What did I want? An automatic profile, or did I have a new one to enter? I adjusted the goggles needlessly, suddenly feeling foolish and vulnerable, concerned that my son might come home early, although I knew that he wouldn't. "Automatic," I said out loud, and a selection of naked women that Blake must have programmed came up. I scanned them for a while, disappointed with his taste, even requested a few more, feeling increasingly invasive, rebellious, and rude. Ten minutes later, I finally did what I had come to do, downloading my picture of us in front of the farmhouse. I remembered running my fingers through Sophia's hair. *Impossible.* I had no voice, no smell, no taste, to feed the computer. *Limits,* I thought, *as if a plane can ever be a bird.*

And then I was there – she was with me – in the picture I'd cherished for so long. *Her face, her eyes.* I started to cry.

* * *

THE LAST TIME I had seen Sophia alive had been three months after I'd moved out and I had ended up sobbing then too. I had arrived by cab on a Saturday afternoon and she was waiting for me on the porch, holding something behind her back. A gift of some sort, I thought at first, until the cab pulled away, and she pulled out a gun.

"You're killing yourself," she said, stepping toward me. "Let me do it fast for you instead." I sucked in air against my will.

"Sophia?" I said, my voice betraying my confusion. "Sophia, put the gun down, please." *She won't shoot, she won't shoot.*

SOPHIA FELT REAL in my arms. The gloves and the helmet and the chair had become imperceptible to me. What I felt was her skin and her hair and her lips. I brushed my eyelashes against her nose, the smoothness shocking me and making me kiss it. From that distant, precious time in my life, my soul mate was back, hugging me hard, like no one does an old woman. Except in the background, I kept noticing that damn dilapidated porch.

"Why are you back?" she screamed at me from the porch.

"I told you I'd come. What's wrong, Sophia? Where's everybody gone?"

"Aren't you worried about them? You left them alone – your precious, grimy children. Don't think you're leaving the little bastards with me."

"You're not making sense, Sophia. It's the drugs making you do this. Put the gun down. We'll spend the afternoon together."

Sophia's head was lowered but her eyes still glowered at me. Her arms were swaying about, the gun now aimed at my crotch.

"You made your choice, you fuckin' saint."

"We've talked about this, Sophia. You would have done the same."

She jolted, the drugs and the anger making her pull up the gun so fast she had to adjust its aim at my head. Her finger clenched near the trigger.

"I wouldn't have? Say it … say it … say it! I never have, you bitch, you know that. Why would you drive him away from me?"

I struggled to make sense of what she meant, desperate for words that would calm her, when her son Joel came out on the porch. He must have come home for the weekend, out of guilt, perhaps. He looked powerful and beautiful, like his mother.

Relief.

Joel would get her under control – but in one dark flash of a moment, the mother spun around and took aim at her son. I flung myself at the porch steps, convinced that she would shoot. My leap landed short and as I scrambled up from my panicked fall, I saw Joel coolly reach out and ease the gun our of her hands.

"You did this to me!" she screamed over and over again, staggering down the porch steps toward me in a now impotent attack. She tripped, her body rolled to the ground, and she lay there in hysterics. Joel looked at her with an expression of disgust and then squatted down on the other side of her, both of us trying to pick her up. His face was a breath away from mine when he said, "My mother would never kill me over a cunt like you."

I left him to carry her up the stairs himself.

WHEN I HEARD Jackie read Sophia's words to me later, they were like bullets shot from the grave. I blamed only myself. She had thrown her vanquished self down the porch stairs at me and I had bowed to the son and walked away.

* * *

AND NOW IN the apartment of my own son, with his spotless kitchen counters and his porno reality room – and Sophia's body so close and so real – I heard again what had been said to me before. Her troubles had been bigger than me. I ran my hands through her wild hair and wished she would speak. All these years I had been haunted by the memory of her and I never loved fully again. I kissed her lips and let myself believe for a moment that she was still alive.

Goodbye.

Twenty years after her death, a voice finally came to me, in that steel box of a room. It wasn't screaming from heaven or hell like she had in her letter. This voice was true and loving, and it was asking for strength and forgiveness – but it wasn't Sophia's voice that I heard. It was my own.

The Sleep Clinic for Troubled Souls

Hiromi Goto

DESDEMONA WAS dying.

Desdemona was dying of loneliness, pure and simple, and when she said so out loud her friends laughed. When her loneliness turned into a refrain, a byline, a daily prayer and invocation, they began clicking their tongues, rolling their eyes, and telling her to stop being so melodramatic. Melodrama, they said, was unattractive, and she would be even less likely to get laid. Why didn't she try an Internet chat room? Her situation was not unlike that of many others in their mid-thirties, they said, and it was nothing a little speed-dating wouldn't cure. Then, her friends avoided her.

Just as well, Desdemona thought. The disarray of her apartment might have slipped over the edge of neglected into the domain of disturbed. But she couldn't be sure. Desdemona scraped her lower teeth over the fleshiness of her upper lip. There was nothing psychotic about being lonely and messy, she tried to reassure herself. So she was behind on a few deadlines. It happened. The letter from the collection agency, however, had been a sucker punch in the gut. How would she keep this shameful situation from her mother and her corporate sister? Didn't collection agencies go after family members if the person in question couldn't pay up? Desdemona scrubbed her palms up and down her face, breathing noisily against her fingers. She felt a large patch of dry skin slough off her left cheek and she jerked her hands away from her face. She watched the piece of herself drift back and forth like a giant snowflake before it fell to the ground. Desdemona shuddered. She furtively glanced around, but no one had witnessed the small death. She crouched down to the sidewalk and snatched up the dead part of her self. She shoved the crêpe-like skin into her mouth. Slightly chewy with a tinge of citrus. Desdemona ate the piece of herself as seriously as if it were a holy wafer.

Just as Desdemona was wiping her guilty lips, a small child wearing a Winnie the Pooh hat and clasping a monkey-shaped purse caught her eyes. Black bangs hung past the bottom of the yellow hat and the dark line slashed across the child's pale brow. She was so cute that Desdemona's heart twanged with a strange sensation, tears filling her eyes. Desdemona blinked and blinked and smiled at the child who tugged imperiously at her father's hand.

The child's eyes locked on Desdemona. "What's that boy doing?" the child asked loudly.

"Shhh," the young father admonished. "He … he doesn't have any money so he's asking for donations."

"Why doesn't he have any money?"

"Maybe he had to leave home?" the father replied, sounding rather doubtful.

"Give him a dollar!" the child demanded.

Desdemona's ears burned. She awkwardly rose to her feet and stuffed her hands in her pockets. Granted, she didn't have a great deal of money, but co-op housing meant she could afford a place downtown and find contract work in women's centres when the writing grants didn't come through. And if she were paid for all of the community work she did for free her net worth would….

"I'm not a boy!" Desdemona spluttered, her cheeks burning in the cold, damp autumn air.

"He's a girl," the child said, wonderingly. "Give him *two* dollars!"

The young father thrust the money toward Desdemona. "Here." His face morphed through complex emotions and ended with a patronizing smile. "We're going to be late." He pulled his daughter's hand.

Desdemona backed away, both palms held outward, as if she were retreating from wild animals.

"Take it!" the child commanded. Her dark brown eyes stabbed Desdemona through and through.

"No," Desdemona said weakly.

"You better," the child warned as she stepped away from her father. She clumsily tucked the tail strap over her arm before unzipping her monkey purse. She shoved her hand inside. Desdemona could hear the rustle of paper, candy wrappers, the clinking of loose change.

Lord, thought Desdemona, the charity case of a child. Could my life be any more pathetic?

The child pointed an orange plastic gun directly at Desdemona's heart.

"You better take it."

Desdemona gasped, eyes darting between the pistol and the young father. The father's mouth dropped open, then he glared at Desdemona.

Desdemona fought the compulsion to raise both hands over her head. "You allow this behaviour?" she asked.

"Well, if you hadn't made a fuss and just taken the money, she wouldn't have gotten her gun!"

A small group of people clustered around them.

"Take the kid's money," a bystander admonished. His small goatee and pork-pie hat were embarrassingly pseudo-Euro. "She's being charitable and generous. Don't squash those virtues."

"What about the gun?" Desdemona said.

"It's true," Pork-pie hat said solemnly. He turned to the young father. "You need to teach your daughter that enforcement is not the answer. We need to teach the world's children to be open and accepting of all ways of being."

"Piss off," the young father snapped at the helpful bystander. "Who asked for your opinion?"

"You're bad," the little girl said decidedly, shaking her head at Desdemona. "I don't like you." She turned away, tugging at her father's hand, her water pistol still clasped in her other fist, the monkey purse dangling from her elbow.

Indignation welled up in Desdemona's chest.

"See!" Pork-pie hat said indignantly, and stalked off.

Desdemona's arms dropped to her sides, mouth agape.

The small crowd that had gathered around the scene started to fade away and Desdemona was left standing by herself again.

"I'm not bad," she whispered. "I'm not bad," she repeated a little more loudly, but the child and her father had already turned the corner and were gone.

A coolness slowly seeped into her heart. Desdemona patted her left breast, looking down at her weathered jean jacket. A small dark wet circle stained the light blue fabric. She had been shot.

"You little shit," Desdemona muttered. She wanted to laugh, but tears welled up in her eyes. A pinching stink wafted upward. For a moment she couldn't place the smell.

Apple juice.

"WHAT'S WRONG with you?" Saskia asked, an edge to her tone. She slid her disparaging eyes up and down her sister's attire, lingering over her sallow, dry skin, her clumpy hair, and the triple bags beneath her eyes. "You look like shit."

Desdemona stared vacantly across the café. The buzz of voices hypnotic as sun-drunk bees … apple juice, frappuccino. Do Italians order "frappuccinos" in Italy? My heart was fine until it wasn't. How old was I when I stopped smoking? I dunno. That shot of energy that simultaneously mellows … should I start again? I don't miss the fights —

"Hello!" Saskia snapped her fingers, twice, in front of her gaze.

"Uh!" Desdemona twitched. "You scared me." Her small red eyes focused on her sister's annoyed face.

"Are you on drugs?" Saskia asked.

"No, of course not! You know how I feel about them!"

"You look and act like you're stoned out of your head," Saskia exclaimed. She angrily stirred her coffee although she hadn't added anything to the cup. "What's your problem? Are you out of money again?"

Desdemona clumsily lurched to her feet, the chair almost toppling backwards as she swung for her jacket.

Saskia wrapped her manicured fingers around Desdemona's skinny wrist. "Okay, okay. Sorry. You just look like a junkie. I'm worried, okay?"

Desdemona grudgingly sat down. "I asked you here because, well, I need some advice.…" The last time she had fought with her sister it had been about Lucy. Desdemona had informed her that she'd rather piss broken glass than listen to Saskia's advice, and then gave her the silent treatment for three months. Desdemona had enough of a conscience that her ears turned bright red.

"You want *my* advice?" Saskia's tattooed eyebrows could not rise because of the Botox treatment, but her tone spoke volumes.

"The sanctimonious one has fallen, I know," Desdemona muttered. "Laugh if you want, but I think I'm in trouble."

"Legal?" Saskia clipped, all business.

"No, no," Desdemona said. She took a gulp of coffee. She shouldn't drink it at all, but she was so tired. Caffeine was the only thing that kept her going during the day. The whir of the cappuccino machine. The merging voices of people talking, laughing, lapping like a wave. The novel was going nowhere. It didn't have a leg to stand on. Did I eat breakfast? My mother made horrible breakfasts. I'm close to finished on the project proposal. Tweak some numbers. That's all. A new computer. A novel ending. Collection agency. Legless. When was the last. The rent –

"Dezzy!" Saskia shook her shoulder.

The use of the innocent childish nickname that had been turned into hateful taunts at school snapped Desdemona out of her stupor. "Don't call me that," she moaned.

"What's wrong with you?" Saskia leaned forward. "Are you sick?"

"I can't sleep," Desdemona said hoarsely. She blinked carefully, but it still felt like grains of sand were embedded in her corneas. "I haven't slept for ten days."

Saskia drummed her hard red nails on the tabletop. "Insomniacs often feel like they haven't slept, but they actually do. It's almost impossible to not sleep at all. Unless you have that prion disease...."

"What –"

"Have you been to your doctor?"

"She suggested I get some counselling," Desdemona said.

"Typical," Saskia muttered, eyes narrowing, "but you've been mopey." She drummed her dark red fingernails on the tabletop. "Ever since that idiot Lucy dumped you. Maybe you do need a shrink."

"Please, can you please stop saying 'idiot' every time you mention Lucy's name? Ten days ago a kid shot me with apple juice. Nothing's been right since."

"What the hell are you talking about?" Saskia snapped.

Desdemona tried to explain the unpleasant incident. How it had triggered something deep and profoundly disquieting. "I used to think I was just lonely. You know, after the break-up and all, but ever since the kid shot me in the heart I haven't been able to sleep. The night stretches out in front of me like a desert. My eyes are grainy and hot, bees buzzing in my head. I can hear every cell in my body, vibrating like a tuning fork. Sleep is like a drink of cool water ... but there's nothing but sand everywhere I look."

"Did you try turning off the lights?" Saskia asked.

"The lights are turned off. The desert is a *metaphor*," Desdemona groaned, and dropped her head into her hands.

"Oh." Saskia rolled her eyes. "You're talking poetry stuff. You must not be that bad off."

"I am," Desdemona moaned. "If the lack of sleep's not enough, I haven't been able to write a thing. Not even a line. And they police the arts grants now. I have to send in the completed project as well as a report."

"You were talking poetry gibberish just now," Saskia pointed out.

"That was all just cliché!" Desdemona grabbed two handfuls of hair.

Saskia's lips turned downward as she stared at her sister. "Look, why don't I get you hooked up with *my* doctor. Yours is probably a leftover hippie. Sometimes cold hard science is the best cure." She pulled a swatch of sticky notes from her purse and scribbled a name and address. She peeled the page off and leaned over to stick the bright pink square on Desdemona's head. "Don't phone first. The receptionist is a freak and my doctor's not accepting any new clients. But if you go in and talk face to face it should be okay. I'll give my doctor the head's up. And shower before you go," she added. "You have dandruff."

"Why did I ask you here again?" Desdemona asked.

"Because you love me most of all," Saskia said, standing up. "And your tree-hugging friends don't know how to deal with you."

Unfortunately, Desdemona thought as she watched her older sister leave, she was right. She then peeled the pink sticky off her head and looked at it. 1266 Carmine Street. She shook her head. She wasn't up to hard science. Cold hard science was probably a man, too. She shuddered at the image that popped into mind. She put the note in her pocket. She'd try more acupuncture, maybe even check in with Lucy's old herbalist in Chinatown. She could pick up some steamed buns at New Town Bakery. Mmmm, they were so cushy and soft and hot, like great white breasts....

"Excuse me. Will you be leaving soon?" Two young men with fashionably rumpled designer shirts hovered over her table, staring pointedly at her empty mug.

Pah, Desdemona thought, to be twenty and naturally arrogant and sexy again. "Yah, sure," she muttered, grabbing her jacket. She didn't even have the energy to slip her arms into the sleeves.

"Did you see her hair," one of the young men whispered.

"She wouldn't be half bad with a make-over," his companion sniffed. "What a waste."

She bought some dandruff shampoo on the way home.

THE FURNACE CLICKED, like a tiny old man was striking flint to metal.

Little old man, little old man —

Whoosh! Desdemona twitched, her heart stopped, only to pound painfully once more. It's only the natural gas igniting, silly. You hear it all the time.

The roar of hot air forced its way through the ducts; she

could hear every mote of dust, every particle of mite droppings buzzing in the air. Desdemona, eyes hot and itchy, stared up at her night-dim ceiling. The streetlight directly in front of her third-storey co-op bachelor apartment shined through the cracks between curtain and frame, casting a dirty orange glow throughout her room.

Determinedly, she closed her eyes.

Her heart bloomed loudly inside her ears like a monstrous night flower. The pulse of blood, awake and noisy. Air whistled in and out of her nostrils, filling her lungs like a meaningless device.

She tried breathing deeply. She was lying in a hammock. A salt breeze coming off the warm sea. A slow, rocking motion.

Her heart would not stop its senseless pounding.

She tried visualizing the relaxation of her body beginning with her toes, the small bones and muscles of her feet, going up, up....

A truck roared by with a belch of exhaust, the stink rising to fill the night air.

Groaning, Desdemona rolled out of bed. When she stood up, her boxer shorts sagged low on her hips. She hitched them up and tried to pinch at the skin around her bare waist. She was losing weight. God, maybe she did have a prion disease!

She knew she wasn't supposed to look, but she couldn't stop herself. Knocking over her long-unused dream journal and a childhood photo of herself and her mother, she reached for her small clock.

4:19 AM....

"Oh, no," Desdemona moaned. She fell into a fit of shivers. Cold. Cold. She shambled through a pile of laundry, heaving T-shirts and dirty socks into another heap until she found her favourite jean jacket. Shrugging into the redolent cloth, she clutched the denim to her bare chest as she stumbled toward the kitchen. She stepped into something icy and wet. Wearily she rubbed the sole of her foot along her shin. She hoped it wasn't pee. Whose would it be?

Desdemona pulled open the refrigerator door and blinked blearily in the cold light. She grabbed the milk and filled a mug, shuffling over to set it in the microwave. She watched the mug spin around, around, around, around, around, around....

Ding!

Desdemona almost fell backwards, her heart pounding with terror. Hands clammy and shaking, she reached for her hot milk. "I'm a wreck," she muttered. "I'm going to lose my mind if it's not gone already." She peeled the skin off her milk and dropped it in the dirty sink. "Don't worry," she whispered. "It's just insomnia. You're not crazy. You just can't sleep." She sipped from her milk; the steam rising from it smelled like her mother. "But look at you," she whispered hoarsely. "You're talking to yourself! You've lost so much weight and you can't focus on those proposals for the centre!" Desdemona shook her head, her thoughts leaping like fleas. "And you have to finish the novel. *I'm scared.* Saskia's never scared. What's that?" Desdemona leapt around. The echo of a knock weighted the air. "It's nothing." Her eyes darted. "Collection agency, ha, ha, ha.... You hated those floral trousers and she made you wear them! You're such a loser. If Mummy ever found out.... No one reads experimental fiction any more. A collection agency is after you! Man oh man. You can try shuffling credit cards. Lucy managed to get by on that. *I dunno.* Idiot! You only have one credit card and it's maxed out! Are there mice in the co-op? That noise. How long are you going to live like a student? Shower, you pig. What do you have to show for yourself? You're thirty-six. Shut up! Shut up!" Unthinkingly she took a big gulp from her mug and hit the hot middle, scalding the roof of her mouth. "Ugh!" she garbled, dribbling milk down the front of her jean jacket. Glumly she stared at the mess. Laundry. She hadn't done her laundry for … she couldn't remember how long. Only that she had nothing left to wear. Sighing, she wiped the spillage off with a smelly dish sponge. Tears filled her eyes as she tongued the bubbles of water trapped beneath a thin transparent layer of skin. Weepy. She was so weepy all the time. She might have been lonely before, but she'd never been weepy. Useless….

She hated her! That apple-juice-shooting child!

Desdemona dumped the remaining milk into the sink and dropped the mug with a clatter. The acupuncture and the St John's Wort weren't working. The lavender bath salts, the massages and acupressure hadn't made a difference. Soothing humpback whale songs, chamomile tea, aromatherapy, meditation, wearing slippers with pokey rubber bottoms, none of it had made a difference. She hadn't fallen into sleep for over a month.

Desdemona shuffled from the kitchen to her bedroom. She clicked on the small lamp on the bed stand and began rummaging through the piles of dirty jeans for the note. She was ready to accept cold hard science.

DESDEMONA squinted as she fought to focus on the doctor's name. There was no making out her sister's loopy writing. The address, however, was legible. 1266 Carmine Street. A drop of rain fell on the pink square of paper and she shoved it back into her pocket, popping open her umbrella as the patter fell into a shower.

The small wet street branched off the busyness of Main. Heavy trees and rows of shrubbery cast a strange stillness upon the area. Older model two-storey houses had been converted into private offices and second-hand clothing stores. It didn't look like the kind of place her sister would frequent, although the area wasn't too far from Saskia's office. Maybe that's why she'd ended up with this doctor.

The rain turned into a liquid wall as Desdemona, bent forward against the onslaught, passed a café. The water dribbled down the large frame window, making the handful of occupants look like figures in a Munch painting. Desdemona needed another hit of coffee, but she would get her hit elsewhere.

1204, 1210, 1242, 1266.

Desdemona stared blearily. Four storeys tall, it was the only brick building on the block. Tiny barred windows were positioned high above ground level. No signs were posted in the small tidy lawn nor hung from the wall next to the heavy wooden doors. *Christie Manor*, however, was hewn into the stone arch high above the entrance. Desdemona shrugged. She reached for the large brass knob and went inside.

The foyer was tinged with the smell of wet wood and mildew. A heavy and ornate light fixture, designed like unwieldy flowers, cast a dirty light on the dank space. A row of metal mail slots ran along one wall and unwanted flyers littered the marble floor. The second set of doors was locked. Desdemona rattled the knob for a few seconds before noticing an ancient intercom. There was only one button and a circular mesh.

Frowning, Desdemona started to turn around to leave. This was weird. But outside the rain was falling straight up and down, with hardly a break between. Desdemona sighed heavily and pressed the button.

Desdemona cleared her throat. "I'm here to, umm, see a doctor." She sounded stupid. She didn't know the doctor's name. "My sister sent me," she added.

The intercom crackled faintly. Someone was listening, but there was no response. Desdemona shook her head. Waste of time. Her joints ached with exhaustion; her shoes were so heavy and the muscles next to her right eye began twitching madly. Her hand shook as she reached for the large brass doorknob to leave.

But then Desdemona heard a buzz and click as a second door was unlatched. She stumbled back in before the button was released and she was locked out again. She pushed through the second doorway and spilled into a dark hallway.

The odour of mildew and mould, infused into the ancient carpeting, was made worse by the synthetic sweetness of floral air freshener. Desdemona's pulse bulged in her temples, and nausea lapped at her throat. Bright lights speckled her vision and suddenly her right arm flailed, her umbrella clattering to the floor. A firm hand was gripping her by the elbow, and an arm was wrapped around her back, leading her swiftly through an office door.

"You're fine. You can sit down. Lower your head." The hand gently pushed Desdemona's head toward her knees. "Take deep, slow, breaths."

Desdemona slowly sucked in air and the nausea passed. "Th-thank you," she stammered, as she sat up. When she looked up, her mouth fell open. "L-Lucy?" she stammered. Even before she'd finished saying her name, however, Desdemona could see that the woman was at least fifteen years older and much slimmer than her beautiful ex.

The woman placed a hot hand to Desdemona's icy forehead. "You must still be groggy."

Desdemona shook her head. "No. You just look like my ex-girlfriend."

The woman raised her dark eyebrows, intrigued.

Desdemona blushed. "I'm not hitting on you," she mumbled. "You look like you could be her older sister."

"Well," the woman said. "I suppose I should be happy I don't look old enough to be her mother."

Was *she* flirting? Desdemona wondered. A wave of exhaustion submerged her as the last of the adrenalin burned off and her spine sagged beneath her body's weight.

"You're not well," the woman said.

"Insomnia," Desdemona slurred. "I need a doctor —"

"How did you hear about our clinic?" the woman asked sharply. "This is a private facility."

"My sister told me,…." Desdemona said weakly. Ahhhh, stupid. This had to be the psycho receptionist. She wished she had spoken to Saskia before coming.

"Your sister is a client. I see," the woman said, a little more warmly. She sat down at her desk, empty except for a single laptop computer and a cell phone. The receptionist sat on her chair, her folded hands on her lap. "Well, if that's the case…. We're trying to compile data on siblings, as a matter of fact. And there's a space for you if you'd like. We just need you to fill out these forms and I'm sure the doctor will be happy to see you."

Desdemona blinked with uncertainty. Something felt off, but she couldn't see what it was. She reached for the sheaf of papers, her hand shaking with fatigue. The print was tiny and she could not read the words. "I'm having a hard time focusing," she said weakly.

"Let me read it for you." The receptionist extricated the forms from her. "Name?"

Desdemona's mouth fell open.

"Name?" the receptionist repeated.

"Desdemona Stone Tamaki."

"Age?"

"Thirty-six."

The woman's neutral voice was rather hypnotic and Desdemona's answers began to spill out even before her brain had registered what was being asked.

"Birth date? Place of birth? Racial background?"

Desdemona's answers slowly filled her mouth and birthed into the air. Her responses floated listlessly like helium balloons.

Dietary habits? Blood type? Chronic illness? Childhood trauma? Do you remember your dreams upon waking? Frequency of masturbation? Your first sexual encounter?

Desdemona shook her head. "Could you repeat that?" she groggily asked.

"Describe your first sexual encounter."

How weird, Desdemona thought. What questions had she already answered? Had she, in fact, disclosed more than she normally would? She couldn't remember. "What does my first sexual encounter have to do with my insomnia?"

"Well, as your sister must have told you, this is a sleep clinic for troubled souls. In order to deal with your insomnia, which is only a symptom, we must pinpoint your 'trouble,' so to speak."

Did Saskia have a troubled soul? Wow, Desdemona blinked sleepily. Saskia had a soul. A bubble of unease floated to the surface. "This isn't a Christian facility, is it?"

The woman laughed. "My dear, not at all. We understand the 'soul' to be much in the same tradition of 'spirit' or 'ki.' When this clinic first opened I wanted to use the word 'spirit,' but Dr Ku believed that North Americans would be more comfortable with soul.'"

"You've come from somewhere else?" Desdemona asked.

"Yes," the woman said.

Unease crawled along Desdemona's skin. She stared vacantly at the glass table, the modern chair, the computer screen, the cell phone. The only other piece of furniture was what she was sitting on, a wooden bench like something out of a nineteenth-century schoolhouse. The small windows set high in the wood paneling behind the desk offered strips of sky between security bars. There was something amiss....

"That's enough for now," the woman said tersely, as if reading her mind. "We can fill in the rest after your session with the doctor."

The receptionist turned toward the wall, then raised her hand and poked something with her forefinger. A door-sized panel slid open, revealing a second room, which makes Desdemona sigh with awe. Maybe Uhura would be on the other side, she thought.

"Everyone loves this door," the receptionist said. "Come this way."

An opaque light filled the inner room, but Desdemona could not make out any details. Her eyes would not focus.

The receptionist, as if familiar with the reaction, cupped Desdemona's elbow. "This way," she said. "There's an examination table directly in front of you."

Desdemona raised her hand and her fingertips brushed against something smooth and cold.

"There's a footstep at your feet. Please take a seat on the table and the doctor will be with you shortly."

Desdemona awkwardly crawled up on the table and blinked blearily. "Do I need to change or something?" she asked sluggishly.

The receptionist laughed. "It's not that sort of examination," she said warmly, as if sharing a joke. "You're going to be pleasantly surprised."

Desdemona frowned. What....

"Just lay back," the receptionist said. "Relax."

Desdemona was not sure if she ought to, but she was suddenly, unbearably tired. Exhaustion pressed her down, flat, feeling boneless and nerveless. She could scarcely breathe.

"Perfect," the receptionist whispered, then left through the Uhura door. Desdemona sank into the cool smooth surface of the examination table, her consciousness leaching away. She should be cold, she thought, but her eyes started to roll backward, as if she had been drugged.

Drugged.

Maybe the air was….

Desdemona tried to swing her arm out, but she couldn't lift it off the table. Her pinky could only make a feeble twitching movement. And that was all.

"Whaaaa…." she croaked.

"Hello," an oddly familiar voice suddenly murmured. "Let's begin."

WHEN DESDEMONA blinked her eyes open, she felt finer than air. The chronic weight of exhaustion no longer sapped her muscles, and her caffeine-pumped mind was no longer jitterey. She was sitting on the schoolhouse bench in the reception area. Across from her, behind her immaculate desk, sat the Lucy look-alike. She was staring fixedly at something on the wall a few inches beyond Desdemona's face.

Desdemona instinctively turned her head to seek out the object of the woman's gaze.

"You took to the session like fish to water," the receptionist enthused.

Desdemona looked back at her. The receptionist was smiling, her shoulder-length black hair gleaming blue under the ugly fluorescent lights. "You're the last client today," she said. "TGIF!"

Desdemona looked for a clock, but the walls were bare except for the dark windows. "What time is it?"

"Ahhh!" the receptionist admonished. "Sufferers of insomnia should not obsess about time. It is the first thing you must let go. And let go of it you will, my dear," she winked.

"How do you arrange appointments, then?" Desdemona was puzzled.

"I see the session worked remarkably well," the receptionist nodded. "It's so rewarding to see."

It was true. Desdemona felt tired, but an un-anxious tired. "I'd like to talk to Dr Ku and thank him."

The receptionist giggled. "You've been talking to Dr Ku all along, silly!"

Desdemona frowned. "Was I hypnotized?" she asked slowly. "I don't remember it."

"You signed the form accepting all procedures," the receptionist said tersely.

"I'd like to see it again," Desdemona said, flustered. Why was she causing a fuss when she felt so much better than she had for over a month?

"Why are you causing a fuss?" the receptionist admonished. "If you're so concerned, I'll have a copy for you when you come in for your next session. As you can see we don't have a photo-copier. It's much too noisy."

"Alright," Desdemona said, somewhat mollified. "When shall I come back?"

The receptionist smiled. "Here, at the sleep clinic, we believe that everyone holds the cure to their own troubles. So you decide when you need another session."

"Could I have the phone number?" she asked, glancing at the cell phone on her desk.

"We don't schedule appointments. Whenever you decide the time is right, that is the time. You only need come to this office."

All of the sudden Desdemona desperately wanted to kiss her. "May I ask your name?" Desdemona asked.

"You may call me Ms Mu."

"Is that Chinese?" she asked.

"No," said Ms Mu.

Dr Ku, Ms Mu. It was rather funny.

"Well," Desdemona said awkwardly, "I'll see you next time."

"Yes, we will. TGIF!" Ms Mu said cheerily, and got up to open the door for Desdemona "Don't forget your umbrella."

Outside it was night now, so completely night that all of the shops were dark and very few people were on the streets. The rain had stopped long ago, as the sidewalks were dry. Desdemona shuddered. How long had she been there? What had been done to her?

But she felt better. She really felt better. She couldn't honestly say she felt rested, nor could she say she felt more energetic, but she felt lighter than she had before. She felt she could rise up to the moon. Everything felt sharp, like an open-blade razor, the autumn breeze metallic. Desdemona seemed to float to the bus stop, where she waited calmly.

She would stop drinking coffee. She would listen to classical music. Wind instruments, preferably.

When the bus arrived, the air brakes shushed.

Desdemona started blinking uncontrollably.

Something about the appointments. What....

But the coalescing thought scattered like motes of a dream.

"Ms Mu," Desdemona mouthed as she watched the cityscape flit past the bus window like rapidly sequenced stills.

She would unplug the telephone.

She would wash her laundry.

She would clean out her apartment.

She would open the curtains.

She would be whole.

THE SUN BLARED through the crack in the curtains. The heat began to sear as Desdemona stood helplessly outside a port-a-potty, her legs crossed as one person after another budged in front of her.

The need to pee was excruciating and the heat was unbearable. Blisters began bubbling on her face, on her hand that was raised for protection.

Why don't you say something, a part of her raged. Don't let them treat you like this. But she was incapable of stopping the thoughtless hordes, who brushed past her as if she didn't exist.

She couldn't hold it in any longer. Her muscles broke against the strain and in horror she felt her bladder releasing. But instead of a rush of hot stinking urine a strange *bulging* strained outward against her urethra, filling her panties and –

Desdemona screamed.

She woke up, the echo of her voice lingering in the air.

She blinked stupidly. Her right hand throbbed with pins and needles.

She had to pee.

Desdemona slid out of bed and almost crumpled to the floor when she stood up. Her legs were like water. She stared at her knees. What was wrong with her?

But the urge was too great; she hobbled quickly to the toilet, shucking her boxers along the way. She desperately sat down, peeing as gratefully as if it were an orgasm.

I had a dream, she thought. I had a dream and remembered it! Desdemona could have wept for joy. She couldn't remember the last time she had dreamt. Long before she fell in love with Lucy.

"Sleep clinic for troubled souls," Desdemona whispered. Even if she didn't necessarily believe in souls, she felt as though her troubles were beginning to leave her all the same. She could dream again. Her luck would change. She suddenly felt lighter, as if her burdens had lifted.

She wiped herself and stood in front of the sink to wash her hands. She caught a glimpse of her own image in the mirror and, for a second, saw herself like a stranger.

That woman was so skinny.

Had she lost more weight?

Desdemona slowly raised her hand to her face and felt her cheek. Her skin wasn't dry, but....

Troubled, she turned away from her reflection. It was nothing. She couldn't rely on appearances, of course. What mattered was how she *felt*. And she felt a lot better than she had for a very long time. She wanted to take a shower. She wanted to go out and catch up with friends.

She turned on the shower and hot steam began filling the air. The moisture clung to the mirror and erased her reflection.

DESDEMONA HUDDLED on her bed in the corner furthest from the door. Something had happened in the time it had taken to complete her shower, and now she was afraid, but of what she hadn't a clue. She couldn't stop her eyes from darting. Things. Things! So many things in heaps. Heaps! Messy. Ugly. Her stomach squeezed tight and painful. You should go out for a bowl of congee. You should pull yourself together. Scattered. So many things scattered throughout her room. Her life. You know better. You're a better person. You're a good person. You should write your dream down in your journal. You can do that. You should clip your toenails. The tiny old man in the furnace. Click. Click. The rattle of bones in the fridge. Shards breaking off icebergs. Mammoths frozen solid. Continental drift. Geographical plates. Dead carcasses. That's redundant. *You're* redundant! Shut up! Shut up! Shut —

Someone shrieked.

Desdemona, her heart frozen solid, took several seconds to recognize the sound. She stared at the machine as her old-fashioned answering machine kicked in. *Beep*.

"Look," Saskia began without even saying hello. "Are you doing better or what? I want...."

Desdemona picked up. "Hi, I'm here!"

"I can't stand that answering machine," Saskia snapped. "I don't know why you can't use voice-mail like everyone else."

"I'm glad you called," Desdemona said. "I went to your clinic yesterday and I got to sleep last night."

"I knew my doctor would be better than yours," Saskia said smugly. "Did you get some drugs?"

Desdemona frowned. Perhaps she had and couldn't remember. She tucked her anxiety away and forced a laugh. "I was so surprised, Sas. I had no idea you believed in souls!"

"What are you talking about?"

"You know, the clinic! And you never told me you had a sleeping problem too."

"You're talking gibberish," Saskia said. "Are you feeling okay? Maybe you need to get the dosage on your meds adjusted."

Desdemona laughed nervously again. "Thanks for phoning, Sas. I'll talk to you soon."

"Wait! I'm not...."

Desdemona hung up on her, then pulled the blankets over her head and curled up into a ball.

The phone rang again, but Desdemona did not pick it up.

"Why did you hang up on me?" Saskia shouted on the answering machine. "What's your problem? You sound like a mental case! Are you listening? I'm going to the doctor with you! You better pick up or I'm phoning Mom!"

Desdemona lowered the volume completely. After a while, the tape would be full and no one could leave messages. She tucked herself into bed again and tried to think about nothing, but her mind was filled with Saskia's anxious-making questions.

Her sister was so maddening. Why couldn't she be nice,

like Ms Mu? "Ms Mu," Desdemona whispered aloud. A three-dimensional image of the lovely Ms Mu formed inside her mind. She was so solid, so physically real she could almost smell the lavender and the tinge of oiliness wafting from her hair, the faint perfume rising from her chest. Ms Mu was a beautiful hologram inside Desdemona's brain and Desdemona was completely mesmerized.

As she stared at Ms Mu, her anxieties seemed to fall away. All of the sudden, Ms Mu rose up, weightless, and spun in a slow circle. Desdemona reached out to clasp one of her ankles, but her hand went right through her, and the vision of Ms Mu disappeared.

Desdemona's heart spasmed with the loss. She felt cold and damp beneath her blankets. And frightfully awake.

She had to see Ms Mu again. And the mysterious Dr Ku. Ms Mu had said that there was no need for appointments, that she was the master of her own cure. She would return to the clinic at first light and continue with the therapy, then everything would be right with the world once more.

The little old man in the furnace started striking his flint to metal. Desdemona was beginning to hate him. "Go away," she whispered. "It's quiet time for girls and boys."

Knock, knock.

It came from the kitchen.

The hairs on the back of Desdemona's neck quivered wildly. She knew the sound was coming from the refrigerator. Desdemona tried to laugh it off. "Who's there? Desdemona. Desdemona who? Desdemona who can't play because it's her bedtime!"

Atoms started vibrating inside the air ducts as an insomniac night bloomed once more.

* * *

"WELL," SAID Ms Mu, "I thought you might return soon."

Desdemona stared at her flawless face. Free of wrinkles and dry patches, Ms Mu's complexion was airbrushed perfection. "I slept well the first night right after the session," she said, "but last night was worse than ever." The floor began slowly tilting beneath her feet and Desdemona took a few hasty steps backwards.

Ms Mu sounded sympathetic. "There, there. We see a lot of that kind of thing. You've come to the right place, darling. Here, we strive to split the patient from their destructive patterns."

Destructive patterns, Desdemona thought. "Split" did not sound very holistic....

"Come into the examination room. Dr Ku will be with you shortly."

Ms Mu led Desdemona toward the Ushuru door. Before she went through, Desdemona glanced upward through the small barred windows. There were dark clouds in the sky. It would rain again.

The opaque light in the examination room filled Desdemona's eyes. It did not blind her, but she could not see. She held out her hand and Ms Mu clasped her fingers, then led her to the table, where she lay on its cool and smooth surface.

Desdemona did not know if Ms Mu had left the room as Dr Ku had entered. Maybe they were both there, staring at her. Maybe she was alone, waiting for nothing and no one. She had no way of knowing. A writhing sensation spasmed somewhere between her stomach and her loins in an excruciating way.

"Oh, lord," Desdemona groaned. What was she coming to? Don't let it stop....

A hand started stroking her brow. Desdemona tried to say something, but slobber trailed down her chin.

"Shhhh," a voice murmured. She sounded so young, and so painfully familiar.... Whoever she was, she *smelled* young too: as redolent with hormones as an animal in rut. A wave of nostalgia washed over Desdemona and her eyes grew wet. To smell this young again, to be ripe and fresh....

What was an adolescent doing there?

"No more questions," the young voice said. "No more answers."

Tears started falling down Desdemona's face. Loss. The unbearable loss.

"Ahhhiii whhant tuh seeeee," Desdemona slurred. She tried to raise her hand to her eyes, but her arm was so very heavy.

Drugs....

"There's nothing to be afraid of," the young voice soothed. "Everything that happens here is of your own making."

Desdemona's thoughts stretched like putty in her mind. Slow, elastic, wrong. Wrongness. She had no control.

"Shhhhh," the young voice murmured. "You actually do. I think this is the key to your conflict. The repression of your own true desire, your fear of asserting your autonomy. You are unable to truly accept yourself."

Desdemona groaned. She hated Freud, with his cigars and his envious penis. She would kill Saskia when she got out of here....

Qualifications. No framed medical diplomas on the walls of the office. That was what was missing!

"Correct." The young voice sounded pleased. "This room is actually a metaphysical bubble, an interspace created by your repressed needs and desires." The young voice chuckled knowingly. "Sometimes we like to call it a Freudian Slipstream. Of course, it starts slipping well past Freud rather quickly."

Desdemona could no longer feel her limbs, and an unbearable weight pressed down on her chest, making it difficult to breathe. She gasped, but her muscles failed her and her throat began to collapse in upon itself. Her eyes rolled inside her slack face. Who else? Saskia. Her soul. Scammers! Quacks! It's your own fault. Fool. No one knows you're here! Mummy.... Drugs. Experimental. But she hadn't paid. Medicare. Can't. Help....

It was too much. Her consciousness plunged into a dark infinity.

DESDEMONA STARED at dim light slipping through the crack between the curtains. The unexpected night. Her heart bulged with terror and she instinctively rolled to her side to dry-heave.

The nausea passed and she laid back, staring at the ceiling.

She had no recollection of coming home.

How do you know you were ever at the clinic? Maybe you dreamed the whole thing?

That would mean I was sleeping.

Didn't you want to remember your dreams?

Desdemona closed her eyes. She wanted to cry, but the inside of her eyelids felt raw and abraded, like she was blinking bits of glass.

An icy chill crept up her body from her lower extremities. Her feet were so cold, they ached. Desdemona reached down with one hand and felt the restriction of heavy clothing. She was still wearing day clothes, even her jean jacket, and everything was damp, her socks soaking wet. Desdemona fumbled for her bedside lamp. Her fingers were numb and clumsy.

She squinted against the glare, needles of pain stabbing her pupils. When she could finally focus, her mouth fell open.

Her shoes lay next to her bed. Mud was tracked over the unwashed laundry on the floor. And in the far corner of the room, a small child sat huddled against the wall.

She was dressed in a navy-blue T-shirt and tan shorts, and

clasped her bare legs with thin arms. She stared at Desdemona, her eyes dark and flat.

Desdemona bellowed with shock and the child jerked upright, as if electrocuted. Desdemona scrambled up, against the wall, and the child sprang from her corner and ran out of the room and down the hallway with dirty bare feet.

She couldn't have been more than four or five.

For a moment, Desdemona could not move. Then she leaped from her bed and chased after the little girl. There was something about her. She'd seen her somewhere before.

"Wait!" she shouted. "Come back. I won't hurt you!"

Desdemona thought she heard a small whimper from the tiny kitchen. Then, a small bang and the clinking of glass.

In the kitchen, a light shone from the open refrigerator, the door slowly swinging shut. Desdemona grabbed the handle and looked around.

The child was not here. The window was closed and the door that opened to the outer hallway was dead-bolted.

Desdemona peered into the fridge, the hair standing up on the back of her neck. Only a glass jar of milk gone bad, a mushy half-head of lettuce.

No child.

Desdemona slammed the fridge shut and groaned. A bad nightmare.

Her mouth dry, she went to the bathroom and, without turning on the light, got a glass of water. She gulped it down and poured herself another. The cold hit her stomach and she started shivering violently. Teeth clattering, she pulled off her wet clothes and left them on the bathroom floor. She took her bathrobe off the hook on the door and wrapped herself tightly in it.

She went back to her bedroom and bit her lip in dismay. Not only was the mud all over the floor, it was on her sheets and blankets. Desdemona pulled the dirty sodden mess from her bed and flung it into the corner where she thought she had seen the child. She pulled a sleeping bag from the closet and zipped herself in.

3:47 AM. Desdemona blinked anxiously.

In the kitchen, the refrigerator began to knock.

Desdemona did not turn off her lamp. She sank lower into her sleeping bag and clutched the material tightly to her chin. That sound, she told herself, is caused by a mechanical malfunction.

She did not close her eyes.

Ms MU SMILED enigmatically. Desdemona, her mouth wet with longing, watched as the beautiful receptionist unlatched a hook behind her neck and her silky dress began to slither downward. A rush of shivers crept up Desdemona's legs. But as the cloth fell off M. Mu's body, her skin rolled off with it. Desdemona stared, unable to turn away. Underneath her dress and skin was a layer of dark coarse fur. Desdemona gagged as she realized that Ms Mu had been an ape all along. Ms Mu was an ape and she had wanted her, she still wanted her –

Rap! Rap! Rap!

Desdemona gasped and woke up with a start, her heart fluttering frantically. She stared, in a daze, at the mess of her room. It was light outside, unusually sunny. She had no idea what day it was. Her muddy bedding was still in a heap in the corner of her room. She was sweating inside her sleeping bag. There was no sign of the child.

Rapraprap! The sound came more urgently.

It was her front door.

Desdemona struggled to her feet and re-knotted her robe. "Coming," she said as she hurried down the hallway. She peered through the peephole and bit her upper lip. Oh lord. It was her mother.

Desdemona could see the top of her red-dyed curls bobbling with agitation. "I know you're there, Desdemona!" her mother said indignantly. "I can hear you breathing! Open this door!"

Desdemona's eyes darted about her apartment. Clothes. Books. Flyers. Sticky notes to herself on the walls. She couldn't even see her desk, let alone her computer. She sniffed the air. Did it smell bad? She staggered to the window and yanked it open, then ran to her bedroom to kick the muddy sheets and blanket beneath the bed. She would kill Saskia. She scrambled back to the door where her mother was rattling the knob.

"What are you hiding?" her mother called out. "What do you have to hide from your own mother!"

With dread on her tongue, Desdemona unlatched the chain and flipped back the deadbolt. She quickly ran her fingers through her hair as her mother pushed her way inside.

"Mummy!" she tried to smile.

Her mother peered suspiciously at Desdemona's haggard face. "You have AIDS!" she accused, and burst into tears.

"Oh lord," Desdemona muttered as she curled her arm around her mother's back. She would kill Saskia today, as soon as her sister got home from work. "Mummy, stop crying. I don't have AIDS!" she shouted as her mother continued to bawl, sobbing and gasping like the time her chihuahua had died of a twisted intestine.

"Really," her mother gulped, "I know you people are proud to be gay, and your parents are supposed to be proud with you, but must you shout AIDS for everyone on this floor to hear?"

An intense feeling writhed in Desdemona's belly, and heat flooded her temples. A metallic clanging, like old-fashioned fire engines, rang in her ears. Desdemona shook her head, but it only made the clamour worse. She closed her eyes to the noise and folded into herself. When she was finally able to look up again, her mother had pulled herself together, although pale blue eyes were wet, and her mascara was running.

"I have insomnia," Desdemona said.

"Insomnia!" her mother sniffed. "Insomnia and migraines are what people who think too much get. When I was young we didn't have time to think and dwell on morbid ideas all day long like bohemians. I worked two night jobs to pay my own way through college and I've never had insomnia or a migraine in my life! They say no rest for the wicked, my girl, and as long as you have – unnatural tendencies – you're not going to have a decent night's sleep. The whole time your father, may-he-rest-in-peace, and I were married, I never had a single night of unrest."

"Really," Desdemona said.

"Hard work and a natural marriage makes things right in the world," her mother continued, her eyes veered towards the heaps of clothing and mounds of books and papers in the room. "And cleanliness! A clean house reflects a clean mind!"

"Mummy," Desdemona begged.

"I really don't know where I went wrong. I really don't," she sniffed. Desdemona bit her upper lip in agitation. Luckily, her mother did not burst into tears again.

"Can I get you some tea?" Desdemona asked.

"Good strong black tea," her mother ordered. "One spoonful of white sugar. Not brown."

"I only have herbal teas," Desdemona said. "And coffee."

"Herbal teas are nothing but weeds. And I only drink Starbuck's coffee. Do you have Starbuck's coffee?"

"No, I have fair trade coffee. It's organic." The clanging in Desdemona's ears was growing louder.

"I'm not thirsty," Louisie said, and started picking up dirty socks. "Give me a garbage bag. I'm going to take your laundry home with me and wash it for you."

"Mummy, you're not listening to me," Desdemona said.

Her mother shrieked as something small and brown zipped across the floor and hid under a pile of paper.

"Cockroaches! Your apartment is infested with cockroaches! My own daughter! Living in filth. You're dying, aren't you!" she accused. "My baby girl. Oh, it's not fair. It's unnatural for a mother to outlive her daughter. I wanted to be a grandmother! I wanted to hold your babies and send them Christmas presents and take them to the zoo. My friend Leila's daughter, Patricia is four years younger than you are and she already has three children. I don't even have one grandchild and now you're going to die!"

"What about Saskia?" Desdemona asked.

"Oh, Saskia!" Her mother flapped her hand. "Your older sister has a *career!* She's a businesswoman and a businesswoman has to live like a man."

Desdemona shook her head at the sheer futility of it all. Something hard and heavy pressed against her throat, but she managed to smile. "Yes, Saskia lives like a man," she agreed. Tell her you have to go somewhere, a cool voice suggested. "Mummy, I forgot I have a doctor's appointment. I'm going to be late if I don't leave right now. I'll call you after I get back."

"I can go with you —" her mother began.

"No!" Desdemona shouted. "I mean, it's like therapy. You can't go with me."

"Are you finally getting therapy? Maybe it will cure your homosexuality. I can wait here for you until you get back and we can go for Chinese food. "

"You can take my laundry instead," Desdemona suggested.

"See!" her mother gloated. "You do need my help! You'll always need me."

Desdemona stared at her mother's face, her clumpy mascara, the tightness around her eyes. "It would be very helpful if you'd do my laundry," Desdemona blinked slowly. It was true, after all.

DESDEMONA SHUFFLED down the street, her hands crammed deep into her pockets. A cold wind settled around her neck and Desdemona shuddered at the dampness. The memory of smoking teased suggestively, a nicotine mirage. She tugged her jean jacket more tightly around her. A smatter of raindrops fell on her face like cold spit.

"*Vhhy dahz yoh muzah cause you so much unxiety?*" A vision of Freud appeared before her, hands clasped behind his back.

"Shut up!" Desdemona said out loud, dragging her forearm over her wet face. Several people veered from her on the sidewalk, casting nervous looks over their shoulders as they hurried away.

A laugh rang out from behind her, and Desdemona felt a hot hand slip through the crook of her elbow and intimately squeeze her upper arm. Desdemona yelped, leaping sideways as she shook off the invasive grip.

The laughter rang out again and Ms Mu, affecting chagrin, raised her red manicured fingers to her lips. "Ms Tamaki," she murmured. "You are certainly in a state of agitation. To whom were you speaking, if I may ask?"

Desdemona looked up and down the street before her eyes returned to the beautiful receptionist. "Are you following me?" she asked.

Ms Mu's eyes widened. "My dear, I'm only walking to work."

"Oh," Desdemona muttered, her ears suddenly glowing red. She had no idea she had been walking toward the sleep clinic....

"Freud," she whispered helplessly. "I was talking to Freud."

"Ah," Ms Mu said knowingly. "The therapy is working. Most excellent. Were you coming for another session?"

Desdemona was about to shake her head no, but a strangled little voice rasped, "Yes."

"Very good," Ms Mu smiled and began walking briskly ahead of her. "I'll run along and set up before you arrive!" She began clipping along at a smart pace, her red heels clicking.

Desdemona didn't like this one bit. But then, what was wrong with a little therapy?

You don't believe in it, that's what!

Desdemona determinedly turned away. She raised her foot to step in the opposite direction, but then a terrible rending pain spread beneath her left breast. It felt as though her heart was slowly being pulled out of her chest. Desdemona clamped her hand over the unbearable sensation, gasping for air, the skies reeling above her head. She could not breathe.

Instinctively, she turned back in the direction of the clinic and the pain slowly began to recede, the dizziness passing. Desdemona blinked anxiously, her hand still clasped to her breast. A prickling inside her chest, as if sharp nails were curled around her palpitating heart, ready to tear once more. What had they done to her? What had they done that she couldn't bear not going back? She did not want to go to the clinic. But you can't bear the thought of not going. Don't do it. You're just scared of getting better. That's not true! There must be something horribly wrong if she felt so compelled. They had given her something and now she was addicted.

"Saskia," Desdemona whispered. Saskia's office was close by. Bossy Saskia could help her out of this mess. After all, she was the one who got her involved in the first place.

But what if Saskia was an addict too?

What were they giving up for the sake of this drug?

Tears slid down Desdemona's cheeks, as she tottered towards the clinic, too fearful of her heart bursting into pieces to contemplate escape. The closer she drew to the clinic, the more her discomfort eased. By the time she reached the door, she could scarcely remember why she had been so distraught.

Ms Mu was seated with a most erect posture behind her desk. Desdemona smiled, but Ms Mu only was expressionless. Desdemona's grin sank. Had she somehow offended the strange receptionist? Her heart began pounding inside her chest, growing louder and louder, thundering inside her ears.

Ms Mu shook her head with disapproval. "Your heart sounds awful," she said.

"You can hear it?" she gasped.

"Dr Ku will be displeased. We may have to accelerate your therapy."

A doubt slowly rose from Desdemona's subconscious as she looked up at the windows high above the desk. A sluggish sun cast a wan light between the bars. Desdemona still could not make out the specific panel on the wall that was the Uhura door to the examination room. "The form...." Desdemona said vaguely. "You were going to get photocopies for me?"

Ms Mu frowned. "You took them home with you after your previous session. Don't you remember?"

Desdemona blinked wearily. She did not remember a thing about her last appointment.

Ms Mu tsked. "I'm certain this is just a minor setback. I can't tell you how people's lives have completely changed after they've completed the program."

Desdemona shook her head. Her head felt so heavy she could scarcely hold it up. "I ... my life was fine...."

Ms Mu raised a fingertip to her mouth and laughed with

delight. "My darling girl," she said, shaking her head as if Desdemona were an unreasonable but adorable child. "We wouldn't be here for you if you didn't need and want us desperately. That is how the sleep clinic came to be."

"I … I don't want this anymore," Desdemona rasped, barely audible.

"Oh, sweetheart." Ms Mu rose from her desk with her arms outstretched and pulled Desdemona toward her arms with steely strength. Her voice was softer and kinder than her mother's voice had ever been, Desdemona thought.

She's been so nice.

Why are you so frightened?

"Why are you so frightened?" Ms Mu asked. "We can help you. You're truly getting better. You're so close to a breakthrough." She gave Desdemona a gentle shake. "Let it all go, my dear. Just let it all go."

Desdemona yawned enormously, her jaw cracking loudly. It was so pleasant being held again. With her head cushioned on Ms Mu's breasts, her fears fell away with the melodious rise and fall of the receptionist's cadence. "You have pretty shoes," Desdemona said. Ms Mu giggled. "That's right, darling. You let that id go!" She released Desdemona from her clasp and slipped her hand through Desdemona's arm once more. "Come along. You're ready for your session now."

Her confident air and firm touch were so comforting, Desdemona thought. She tilted her head and let it rest on Ms Mu's shoulder.

"That's right," the beautiful receptionist said softly.

The Uhura door slid open and just as Desdemona stepped through the portal, a tiny shard of awareness pierced the muddiness of her brain with surgical precision.

The windows that let the sunlight into the office were in the *same wall* as the door to the examination room.

She was entering a room that defied all physical rules of being.

Desdemona moaned, all of the sudden incapable of forming words. She tried to stop her feet's senseless movement, but Ms Mu's grip tightened as she resolutely directed her into the chamber.

"Great rewards are to be gained from facing your demons," she said. "Maybe today will be your breakthrough day!" Ms Mu chirped, her grip steely.

Desdemona shuddered as the opaque light blinded her once more. Her teeth were actually chattering with fear, and her movements were distorted, torpid, and senseless, as if her body and reality were stretched beyond reason.

"Hop up!" Ms Mu said cheerily. Desdemona could hear the *thump thump* of her hand on the examination table.

Why wasn't Ms Mu affected by the stretch of time? Desdemona tried to shake sense into herself, but her head was as heavy as a church bell. The slow and deep ringing grew into unbearable pressure, the thin membranes inside her ears bulging outward, warm rivulets of blood trickling out her nostrils.

Ms Mu chided her as she dabbed the blood away. "You're thinking too hard, aren't you!" she admonished. "Don't fight the treatment, darling. You're only fighting yourself. Let go of everything you think you hold dear. And that includes your thoughts!" She slid her hands under Desdemona's armpits and boosted her up, then placed her palm directly above Desdemona's chest and pushed her backward. Desdemona felt like a large senseless beast being led to slaughter.

"N – no," Desdemona said dully. She tried to bat Ms Mu's hand off her chest, but her senseless limb felt like a joint of meat from the butcher's shop.

Desdemona stared vacantly at her arm. Move, she willed. Move! As she did, she slowly realized that she could see again. The opaque light was no longer blinding, though the glare was bright enough to render the open doorway a dark rectangular shadow.

Desdemona laboriously looked up at Ms Mu. The receptionist whipped away from Desdemona's gaze and marched toward the exit. As she drew further from the table, Ms Mu's receding form began slowly shrinking. She seemed to walk away for an excruciatingly long time, and she grew smaller and smaller, until it seemed that she was standing at the far end of a football stadium. Ms Mu turned around and although Desdemona could no longer make out her face, she could see the beautiful woman raise her hand to her mouth.

"You're being naughty!" Ms Mu shouted, her voice now tiny, scarcely audible across the great distance. "There's going to be trouble if you try to resist!"

Was she threatening her? Cold sweat slid down Desdemona's face as she helplessly watched Ms Mu disappear through the door.

"Don't be frightened," a young voice admonished. "Don't struggle. During REM sleep, our brain releases a chemical that inhibits movement so we're prevented from physically acting out our dreams."

A rush of goose pimples spread over Desdemona's skin. She could not see the unwholesome child. Where was she?

The child's voice was so very young. Much too young to know anything about REM sleep.

The brain chemical, unhappily, did not still Desdemona's mind. Then I'm asleep after all, Desdemona decided. I can't move because I'm in REM sleep. So everything that happens here is in my mind, and it's not going to affect me when I wake.

The young voice sighed, resigned. "Think what you like. I'll just do what has to be done."

A small hand patted her arm. Every cell in Desdemona's body shrieked. She saw a clumsy child trying to clamber onto the foot stool, drawing closer to her supine form. The girl, now clinging to Desdemona's arm, was looking down to place her feet. Desdemona stared, wild-eyed, at the top of the child's head, and the shiny black hair that covered her face. As the child looked upward. Desdemona's heart stopped. Every living mote stilled in unbearable stasis.

In the silence of stilled blood, Desdemona finally understood.

"I'm Dr Ku," the sweet child smiled. She had a pageboy haircut and her baby teeth were small and even inside her bright red lips.

Her breath smelled sweet, like rotting leaves.

The child.

An aerial image of her own filthy bedroom bloomed inside Desdemona's mind. Helplessly, she swooped downward, and stopped suddenly in front of her cluttered bed stand.

A framed photo.

In the image, Desdemona was in her mother's arms. She was three or four years old, her pageboy haircut making her large head look even larger. Her mother was on her knees behind her, draping her arms affectionately over Desdemona's little shoulders. They both faced the photographer, maybe her father? She couldn't remember. But in the glare of the flash, her mother's eyes were small and tight with an adult suffering Desdemona had never noticed. Her child self, ignorant of her mother's pain, smiled joyfully at the camera with a face suffused with love....

The child in the photo stood before her now.

Desdemona's heart stammered inside her chest, and her consciousness plummeted into a deep open well. From the fathoms of darkness, the child's face looked like a tiny and distant moon.

"Oh, don't you do that!" her three-year-old self admonished.

Please, Desdemona prayed. Give me the light that blinded me before.

"Look at you!" her child-self scolded. "Repression, repression, repression. It's a wonder how you ever managed to come out!" She giggled, and Desdemona's skin convulsed with disgust.

No, Desdemona thought. Some things weren't meant to be seen … some things must never be seen.

"This is just the beginning!" her three-year-old self said cheerily. "What do we have here?" Her three-year-old self stuck her small arm inside Desdemona's chest, up to her elbow. Desdemona could feel her fingers curl around something and start drawing upward. There was no pain. Her senses were dulled; all she could feel was the horrific tug, tugging, the catching and snapping of irregular pieces….

Helpless to stop her, Desdemona watched her child self gleefully raise two handfuls of something white and viscous, which she flung to the ground and then reached into Desdemona's chest for more. As the tugging and ripping continued, Desdemona's head lolled sideways, her eyes wide and unblinking. How awful, she thought, from a great distance, the insomnia is really the tip of the iceberg….

The air around the young child started to bubble, bulging, convulsing with cells and time. Matter expanded and a thirteen-year-old self and a twenty-year-old self took their places beside the young child. They too slid their hands into Desdemona's chest to fling every bit of her into the world.

Desdemona stared with eyes dry and burning.

The twenty-year-old self smirked. "You let yourself go, no muscle mass to speak of. Didn't we decide in college that we'd never do that?"

The thirteen-year-old sneered. "She doesn't even have the guts to fight! Ha, ha, guts! Get it?"

The twenty-year-old elbowed the teen in the ribs and the girl rolled her eyes. "Bitch," she muttered.

Desdemona was growing faint. She could feel the outer surface of her skin growing permeable, translucent, as more and more of her being was strewn throughout the room. It was growing crowded as all of her many selves drew around the remains of the body, jostling, muttering, murmuring, and giggling. Soon, one last vicious tug would snap the final membrane that tied everything together.

What would be left? Who would be left? Who was in charge? Desdemona tried to laugh. She would have been hooting if she had been capable of it.

The crowd gathered about her was jostled about as a determined child worked her way to the front.

"Hey!" some of the older selves said.

"Let the kid see," another self said. "Last chance in this lifetime."

The child wriggled through until she stood, panting, next to Desdemona. The child self stared expressionlessly at her.

It was *her*.

The child who had run from her bedroom....

She was so stupid. Why hadn't she recognized herself before? She used to love that navy blue T-shirt so much, her mom had to take it off her while she slept.

Desdemona tried to smile. This five-year-old self. She loved her. She used to stare at snails for hours, watch the dew drying on cobwebs, press her ear to the ground to listen for worms. She was the self who had stopped talking for six months because she was so angry at her parents for forcing her to go to school, her older sister for laughing.

I love you, Desdemona thought. *I love you!* She thought

fiercely with every atom of her being. *Of all the selves that deserve to be loved and cherished, I love you the most.*

Desdemona gritted her teeth. Her fingers curled slowly, with excruciating determination, into fists. *I don't want to lose you*, she screamed inside her mind. *I don't want to lose us.*

But only a whisper of air escaped her lips.

"Look, she's finally fighting!" a young voice jeered.

"She's crying!" another exclaimed. "Isn't that sweet?"

A tear trickled into her mouth, salty. She knew it was too late. There was barely anything left in her to call her own.

I'm sorry, she thought. *I'm sorry*, she told her selves. *I should have loved you all. And I didn't know.*

The five-year-old self tilted her head to one side, then forced her way back through the crowd.

Don't go, Desdemona wept. *Come back.*

"Well now," Ms Mu's voice cut through the dense crowd. "This is more like it! This is the kind of client participation we all dream about! You're so clever." The receptionist gently pinched Desdemona's cheek. "I knew you had it in you," she said.

In the final moments, the last door opened.

Ms Mu was an aspect of herself, too....

"Clever indeed," Ms Mu hissed and pinched Desdemona's cheek once more, hard enough to leave a bruise.

Ms Mu who looked like Lucy's older sister ... it wasn't about Lucy at all. It had never been about Lucy. Why couldn't she have seen it earlier?

Not too late, Desdemona thought desperately. *If this –* place *comes from me, then I can make it go away. I can make myself be me....*

But nothing changed. *Your mind can think the thoughts*, a cool voice said, *but your will to act has fled.*

Tears welled in Ms Mu's eyes. She looked unbearably beautiful, like a tragic heroine in a Wong Kar-Wai film. "It hasn't been easy for me." Ms Mu's voice did not break, but Desdemona watched two tears slide slowly down her cheeks.

Ms Mu, Desdemona thought. *Ms Mu, I'm sorry. I can learn to love you, too.*

"It's too late," Ms Mu said matter-of-factly. She wiped her tears away with her pinky.

"Hey," one of the older selves spoke up. This one was in her early thirties, the beginnings of bags lining her eyes. "What about us? You don't speak for all of us."

"Yah," a twenty-something self said hotly. "It was interesting to finally see everyone all together, but what's all this talk about 'too late'? Too late for what?"

The other selves began muttering, jostling with annoyance and agitation.

Ms Mu clapped her hands sharply like a kindergarten teacher controlling a roomful of naughty students.

"Isn't it obvious?" Ms Mu said. "All non-essential, non-active members must be let go."

"Let go?" the twenty-something self shouted. "Let go? We're not a factory! You can't just let go pieces of identity like we're labourers who aren't meeting quotas!"

"That's precisely what must be done," Ms Mu replied. "Otherwise we wouldn't be in this situation. If there was no need for this, it wouldn't be happening at all."

"What kind of loony talk is that?" a thirty-two-year-old self asked. "And who's supposed to decide who is essential and non-essential? I don't know why you think you're in charge, but I, for one, will not let you go through with this."

A murmur of outrage eddied about the room.

"I'm in charge," Ms Mu declared, "because I'm the strongest!" Before she had finished speaking, she leapt atop the thirty-two-year-old and clamped one hand over her skull. Ms Mu's hand seemed to grow larger, wider, covering the top half of the struggling self's head. Before the thirty-two-year-old could wrestle Ms Mu off her back, the receptionist crushed the woman's skull as easily as if it were a desiccated egg.

Oh, Desdemona gasped, as something dear and vital was snuffed from her life.

The younger selves screamed as they ran madly about the room, looking for places to hide. The babies wailed and gasped, their helpless feet kicking at the air, in danger of being trampled. The older selves roared in outrage and surrounded Ms Mu, a mob ready to tear her to pieces.

Ms Mu, perfectly composed, began to laugh.

The mob of selves, enraged by her merriment, inched closer, fists clenched with fury. Ms Mu tipped her head back, her eyes ecstatically shut, as her white skin started to turn red. Then Ms Mu started growing in size.

At the same time, Desdemona could only watch as her various selves slowly began to shrink. The smallest ones were the first to notice, and their forlorn wails echoed inside the room. The twenty- and thirty-somethings stared at the shrinking babies and toddlers, then anxiously peered down at their own receding bodies.

Goodbye, Desdemona thought. *I'm so sorry.*

"What the *hell* is going on? *Oh my God!*"

For a moment, Desdemona could not place the painfully familiar voice.

A small child burst toward them, dragging an adult by the hand. The child was her five-year-old self, in the rumpled navy blue T-shirt. She was panting, her bangs plastered to her forehead, her expression ferocious.

The adult was Saskia.

Saskia, in a beautifully tailored gun-metal grey suit. A lavender Hermes scarf loose around her neck. She spun about, her Botox face revealing nothing as she desperately tried to take in her surroundings, but for the first time in her life she was utterly speechless. She gaped at the many variations of her younger sister who were slowly shrinking right before her eyes.

Desdemona, too drained to speak, was only capable of shifting her eyes between her sister and Ms Mu, who was now nearly six feet tall. Saskia, in shock at the multiple incarnations of her younger sister, had not noticed Ms Mu at all.

The five-year-old child in the navy blue T-shirt tugged at Saskia's hand. She pointed at one of the infants who was trying to raise herself upright. The baby had shrunk so small she was scarcely larger than a squirrel.

The five-year-old child scampered to the infant and clamped her arms around her middle. The baby shrieked, kicking her feet frantically.

"What are you doing?" Saskia asked sharply, sounding more like herself. "Leave that baby alone. We — we'll call social services," she said determinedly.

A tinkle of laughter echoed in the Freudian chamber.

Saskia spun toward the source. Her eyes narrowed. "You!" she sneered. "*Lucy!* I'm *so* not surprised. What have you done to my sister!"

"Darling," Ms Mu reached out to stroke Saskia's scarf, but her sister stepped aside and averted her touch. "You're confused. I can see the family resemblance."

"Shut up," Saskia snapped. "You're not coming back into my sister's life, you freak! Get the hell out of here!"

"I'm afraid it's much easier for you to get out of your sister's life than for me to," Ms Mu sighed.

Saskia did not deign to reply. Without a word, she pounced on Ms Mu, her red fingernails curled into claws. Ms Mu, swiftly as a cat, met her in midair.

Desdemona stared in disbelief. She could not stop them. They scrabbled and rolled upon the floor, knocking over the shrinking selves who wailed as they tried to crawl away.

Desdemona's eyes rolled upward. She was dizzy, as if she were on the floor with them. Thinner. Her ties were growing thinner, finer, and she hardly cared about the outcome. Saskia or Ms Mu, what did it matter? Stillness was better and if the last ties snapped, then everything would be still....

A small hand grabbed hold of Desdemona's chin and shook hard.

Go away, Desdemona thought blearily. *Leave me alone.*

But the persistent hand continued. Wearily, Desdemona opened one eye.

The child. The child who had found Saskia. Her eyes were ablaze with emotion, a shrunken baby dangling from one arm. The squirrel-sized infant kicked her heels, her face purple with rage. She had cried herself voiceless.

The five-year-old self raised the tiny baby high in the air, then lowered her toward Desdemona's chest. The baby sank into her ribs like water into soil. As the infant slowly seeped downward, she stopped her voiceless shrieking, her complexion waning red, then pink, as she tucked a tiny thumb into her mouth and closed her eyes. She submerged completely and Desdemona was left with a mild tingling in her fingers.

The determined child ran toward another baby, slightly bigger than the last, and raised her to Desdemona's midriff. She dropped her unceremoniously and the infant splashed into Desdemona like a stone in a pond.

Ms Mu shrieked. "Those are mine!" she screamed as she struggled to her feet. Saskia tackled Ms Mu around the knees and brought her down again. As they rolled about the floor, pummeling each other, the five-year-old darted past them, desperately gathering up all of the selves. After she tossed in the last of the babies, she started on the toddlers, but once they saw the first one go in, they lined up on their own and took turns plunging back into Desdemona.

And as each self returned, her body tingled with blood and hope. Spirit. She opened and closed her fingers, turning her head from side to side.

Saskia was winning. She was on top of Ms Mu, pinning her shoulders down with her shins, her hands clamped down on Ms Mu's wrists. Ms Mu tried to knee Saskia in the back, but when that proved fruitless, she began bucking her abdomen. Saskia held on tightly, clamping her legs around Ms Mu's waist. They were both panting on the verge of hyperventilation.

"Hurry," Desdemona said hoarsely. "Hurry. Come back."

In a flurry, the shrunken child and teenaged selves mobbed about Desdemona's supine body and leapt back inside like they were hopping into a swimming pool. Desdemona could almost hear the splashes. And as each self returned the vigour returned to her limbs, her senses shivering awake, acute and vital.

"No," Ms Mu wailed, as the adult selves took their turn leaping into Desdemona's chest.

"It's not too late to go to the gym," the twenty-year-old self took the time to say, elbows propped on top of Desdemona's ribcage as the rest of her body dangled somewhere deep inside Desdemona's chest. The young woman winked. She pushed off Desdemona's chest like it was the side of a swimming pool, and clapping her hands together high above her head, she slowly sank out of sight.

Show-off, Desdemona thought.

One after the other, the remaining adult selves returned to Desdemona's body. The last self, hardly distinguishable from her current self, stared sternly into Desdemona's eyes. "It's not too late for change," she said.

Desdemona blushed, then nodded furiously. Her selves – they knew everything about her.

"I – I think I can. I will." Desdemona wanted to look away from herself, but didn't. "I promise," she said.

The last self stared for a few seconds longer, then smiled a crooked grin. "I love you," she said. "We all love you."

Hot tears rolled down Desdemona's cheeks. "Yes," she wobbled. "I love you, too. Thank you."

The last self nodded and stepped back inside. Desdemona took several deep breaths. She sat upright on the examination table and caught sight of the child in the navy blue T-shirt sitting on the foot stool, her hands folded beneath her chin. With her job done the child looked dejected. Saskia was straddled across a rapidly shrinking Ms Mu, whose limbs flailed loosely, like tails on a kite, her mouth open in disbelief.

"Ugh!" Saskia exclaimed, then scrambled off Ms Mu's body, frantically rubbing the germs off her hands against her skirt. "Holy shit!" she shouted as she stared down at Ms Mu, now no larger than a cocker spaniel. Red scratch marks swelling on her forehead, she then turned toward her younger sister.

Desdemona nervously bit her lip as she crawled off the examination table. "Ah…" she started.

"I don't want to hear it!" Saskia snapped. "I have no fuckin' clue what just happened and I don't want to know. Let's get the hell out of here!" Her voice was on the edge of hysteria. Saskia looked wildly about for the exit and caught sight of the child who had come to fetch her. "And Mom's gonna crap when she sees you have a kid. I can't believe how much she looks like you did! How did she ever find you? Or did you look for her?"

Desdemona searched for words to explain, but a hot little hand slipped inside her palm and Desdemona looked down at her five-year-old self. The child did not give anything away with her eyes, but her face was stiff with emotion.

Desdemona crouched down low, and she leaned toward the child's ear. "Do you want to stay outside and play for a while longer?" she whispered.

The little girl remained silent. She nodded her head.

Desdemona hugged her fiercely before she remembered that she had hated it when adults were overly familiar. "Sorry." Desdemona laughed, embarrassed.

Her five-year-old self shrugged, and she awkwardly patted Desdemona's arm.

"What's your kid's name?" Saskia asked.

Desdemona frowned. What had been her imaginary name?

"Yuriko," Desdemona said. "She's Yuriko-chan."

"Cute," Saskia decided. "Let's get outta this place, kid. I'll buy you a frappuccino. I'm your aunt Saskia."

Desdemona rolled her eyes. Her sister had already swept the whole thing her carpet. She supposed it wasn't a bad way of coping, as long as her sister did an annual spring-cleaning.

"You go ahead. I'll be right out," Desdemona said. "I – I have to say something to, ah, Lucy before I go."

Saskia's eyes narrowed. She gently felt the scratch marks that were puffy and red on her forehead. "If I end up with scars I'm going to sue the bitch," she hissed, then grabbed hold of the child's hand, and she marched out of the strange room.

Desdemona's legs wobbled when she tentatively stepped toward Ms Mu. Desdemona took a deep shuddering breath and exhaled slowly.

Ms Mu stared up at her resentfully.

Desdemona blinked. What was she to do with her?

"I suppose you think you've won this round," Ms Mu spat out.

Desdemona frowned. "I don't know," she said slowly. "Do you think so?"

"Now we're all clever, are we?" Ms Mu sneered. "Now we're playing mind games and trying to answer questions with questions!"

Desdemona sighed. "I know you don't like me. That's obvious. But we have to work something out."

Ms Mu turned her head away, her arms crossed over her heaving chest.

"Where else can you go?" Desdemona asked softly. "How long can you exist like this, away from me?"

Ms Mu did not answer, and angrily drew her arm across her eyes.

"Come on," Desdemona said. "Let's go. We're hungry. And we really need to get some sleep."

Ms Mu still refused to speak. Desdemona took a deep breath and draped her arm around her tiny shoulders. "I need you," Desdemona admitted.

"I want to do things *my* way sometimes!" Ms Mu's voice cracked.

"Yes," Desdemona nodded. "I should do things your way, too."

Ms Mu sniffed. "Well, then." She tugged the bottom of her shirt and smoothed down her skirt. "I want to buy some red shoes."

"Red shoes. First thing after I eat something and wake up from a long nap," Desdemona promised.

Ms Mu nodded slightly as she ran her fingers through her hair. She placed her hand directly above Desdemona's heart. "Lie down," she said intoned.

Desdemona lay back.

Ms Mu then stood on top of Desdemona's chest and slowly began sinking inside.

She was still beautiful.

"Don't make me come back," Ms Mu warned.

Desdemona nodded solemnly. "Do you love me, Ms Mu?" she asked wistfully.

"I'll never tell." Ms Mu smiled like a cat. Then disappeared.

* * *

Saskia was waiting outside, tapping her toe on the concrete walkway. The child was on the neat lawn, staring up at bare-limbed trees.

"Did you give that idiot Lucy a good slap?" Saskia asked.

"No, I didn't," Desdemona said. "We just talked. You know how I feel about violence."

Saskia jerked her thumb at the brick façade of the building. "How'd you ever end up at this quack dive? I can't leave you alone for a minute!"

Desdemona glared at her sister. "*You* sent me here! Carmine Street. On the sticky note. Remember?"

"My doctor's on Carmen Street. On the west side!"

Desdemona closed her eyes and shook her head. A strangled noise escaped her lips.

Saskia grabbed her by the shoulder and shook hard. "Don't you dare lose your marbles on me!" she snapped. "You have your daughter to think about now, not just yourself! Mom's gonna *love* this. First you have to be a *lesbian*. Then, a *writer*. And *now* it turns out you've had an illegitimate child! You're some piece of work."

Desdemona stared at her older sister. She loved Saskia, but she did not like her.

Saskia turned toward her niece. "Come on, kid," she called. "You're mom's a nutcase, but she means well. You can stay with your aunty any time you like. I have my own condo and car. Do you like pretty dresses?"

But the child ignored Saskia and tugged the sleeve of Desdemona's jean jacket.

Desdemona looked down into the child's dark, expressionless eyes. The tiny hairs on the back of Desdemona's neck began to rise, one by one. "Yuriko-chan?" she asked hoarsely.

The girl tilted her head to one side.

Would the child ever speak?

What would she say?

Yuriko's lips slowly parted, then her mouth cracked open and an odour of ancient decay ballooned from it.

Desdemona took a step backward.

The child was smiling. And her teeth….

Desdemona's breath lodged in her throat.

The child's teeth were brown. Rotten. Cavities pitting holes into what was left of her enamel.

Desdemona shook her head.

She couldn't remember ever having rotten teeth. She couldn't remember. She was sure she only had one filling. How could this child, her childhood self, have something she never had?

Who was she?

The child closed her mouth over her dying teeth. Her eyes were flat.

"Holy shit," Saskia whistled. "That's going to be some dental bill. I guess she didn't luck out with foster homes."

Desdemona, ignoring her sister, cleared her throat and swallowed hard. She held the child's unfathomable gaze. "Thank you for getting Saskia. That was really clever."

The child shrugged.

Saskia glanced at her watch. "I've got to get back to work. They're going to kill me. I can give you a ride back to your place, I guess. Another half hour won't make a difference at this point."

Desdemona looked at the child, who thought for a moment, then shook her head. She clasped Desdemona's icy cold hand." We prefer to walk," Desdemona said slowly.

"Walk?" Saskia gasped. "It's at least a mile away!"

Yuriko-chan dropped Desdemona's hand and started skipping ahead down the sidewalk, making sure to land upon each and every crack. The child did not look behind her. She skipped and hopped, her hair flying, her small feet stamping down to break every back. Desdemona broke into a run after her.

"You're welcome!" Saskia screamed after them. "Thank you, Saskia, for bailing me out again!"

Desdemona, panting, could scarcely hear her. She and Yuriko-chan would get some lunch. They would have a nap. They would go to her mother's house to pick up the laundry, but mostly to surprise her.

Desdemona's lips quivered. She didn't know if she could bear it.

The Beatrix Gates

Rachel Pollack

DO YOU REMEMBER cancer? In the old days, people fought long, heroic battles with it, usually in scorched body campaigns. Destroy enough tissue and the cancer will run out of food and shrivel away. When the original Nano Factory came up with the first cancer nannies, the designers gave them to doctors who fitted them out like miniscule robo-soldiers and sent them off to war. Cut and burn. Cell by cell. Retake the ground and wall off the infected village, kill the organs in order to save them.

Then it struck someone. Maybe we'd misunderstood cancer. Maybe cancer was the body's desire to become immortal. Cancer cells refused limits, refused to decorously die, they invaded wherever they could go, wherever the medical empire couldn't firebomb them. So over the outrage of the doctors, the Factory (already partly in the hands of the Revolution) began to send in nannies to run with the cancer insurgency. See what cancer really wanted, see how we could use it to overthrow the body's commitment to limits and death. Out of this campaign came the Immortalist program, with all its possible bodies no one ever thought of.

The someone who first saw all this was Annie O, one of the Ancient Trannies, that group of us who managed to survive the rapturous leap into the new world of unlimited nano-transformo. In the old days, Annie was the secret king of America.

A homegrown Kansas trannie, a Colourado Biber Baby (named
for the cowboy doctor and his sex change clinic in the Plains
town of Trinidad), Annie had a brief career as a transgender terrorist before she discovered the Hijras of India, the world's oldest ongoing trans religion. She arrived in Delhi just as Hijras
were starting to win seats in Parliament under the platform "Men
have fucked up and women too, so why not try something else?"
Like some sort of trannie anthropologist, Annie came to film and
take notes. She stayed to put on a sari and dance in the streets.
She'd already passed the Hijra initiation test – "made the cut,"
as someone once put it – and the Hijras embraced her American
trans-formed body, sending her back as king to an America that
had no idea it needed one.

Annie could see cancer in a different way because she understood desire: the desire to die and the desire to live, entwined
like two snakes around a tree older than the world itself. This is
the trannie secret, that we are not just willing to die, we long for
it, passionately, as the pathway to life. Cut open, emptied out,
boiled and cleaned and reassembled. These are old stories, from
long before the Nanochine Society took over the Factory and began to get it right, creating new people out of old longings.

Do you know about the birth of Aphrodite? Ouranos, the
Sky, was hurting the Earth, Gaia. Actually, he was suffocating her
and killing all their children. Clever Gaia managed to save one
of their kids, Kronos, and as soon as he was old enough, Mom-
ma gave him a stone sickle and told him to take care of Daddy.
Kronos didn't go for Pop's throat. He aimed further down and
cut off Ouranos Jr. and threw it into the sea. Ouranos gave up
after that. The Sky pulled back a safe distance from the ground,
crossed only by birds and rockets, neutrinos and weather nanos.
But those missing pieces – they stirred up a torrent of foam on
the water and out of that foam stepped Aphrodite the Passionate.
This is a very old story.

Here is another one. Osiris, gentle God of Egypt, inventor of beer, brother-sister of Isis (who Is and is, forever and ever), lover of sister Nepthys, the Goddess of alchemical mud, Osiris was also brother and brother-in-law of Set, a nasty piece of work if ever there was one. Jealous like Iago, Set chops his brother into fourteen pieces and hides them all over the world. Isis, never one to give up easily, searches up and down the old creation until she can reassemble her jigsaw puzzle husband. Only there's one part missing: a hungry fish has gulped down the penis and dropped down to the oozy black at the bottom of the Nile. So what's a wife (and sister) to do? Isis creates the world's first – everything in myth is first, that's the point of myth – Isis creates the world's first strap-on. With the help of a God named Thoth, inventor of writing, science, magic, and Everything Worth Knowing, this wooden cock crows Osiris back to life.

This is what we mean when we say "sex change." Ripped apart, cut to pieces, and put back together. You have to want it. All of it.

And Thoth, the God of geeks – if the name sounds familiar, it should. You know the ibis nano-tattoo on the upper thigh that marks someone as a member of the Nanochine Society? You know how some nons talk about fucking a trannie as "entering the Palace of the Ibis?" That ibis is Thoth. The Egyptian scrolls depicted the God as a bird-headed techie writing on papyrus. Sometimes the old Gods don't die, they just keep busy until humanity catches up with them. In the ancient world, Thoth revived the dead, he taught the secret sciences, he steered the boat of heaven through the sky and the dark underworld. Sound familiar? When the nannies launch their expeditions into your cells, it's Thoth who guides them. When you pass through the nano Cloud of Unknowing, and you hear that distant flutter of wings, that's Ibis-Thoth.

Dismemberment. Trans (trance) formation. The desire to

die is the desire to live. Cancer, the desire to live forever. It took a trannie terrorist street dancer to see it.

As they say in the Society, let's not beat around the burning bush (and if you can't figure out a bush that burns without being consumed, well, honey, there may be no hope for you). The nons – the non-transsexuals – who first built the Factory, wanted their nan-o-ma-chines to make them *better*, to cure their sicknesses and keep them young, and make everyone pretty, but not actually *different*. They didn't want to stop being who they were, or thought they were, to become something seriously new. And they didn't understand why their tiny machines seemed to come up against unexpected limits, why nothing really worked. That's when the Society took shape, for the trannie Ghost Healers (as they called themselves) understood that these manufactured machines were not robots at all. They were the elementary particles of desire.

A True Story of the Past
As I write this, I am 108 years old. I do this now because 108 is a special number, 1/240th of the Great Year, the time it takes for the constellations to make a complete rotation around the earth. But hey, who's counting? Apparently, only us Ancient Ones, the refugees from the Old World who managed to sail across the Nano Sea into the land of forever. We came to consciousness in a different world, marked by life spans and decay, birthdays and fixed identities. My lover, Callisto, a bright singer in nano-paradiso, likes me to tell her stories of those days. She says it reminds her that everything – including the nannies who release us from form and limitation – all come from the dust of dead stars. So here is something that happened long ago, in the year 1972, Old Calendar.

I was living in London back then, a baby pre-op (as we used

to say in those days of scalpels and drugs), and I and my girl-
friend held a trannie open house on Tuesday nights. For a while
a Japanese woman named Reiko was one of our regular visitors.
Truth is, Reiko wasn't really her name, I don't remember it, it was
so long ago. Reiko is the name of a friend of mine who gave me
permission to transplant her name into my memory.

Truth is, Reiko wasn't really a woman, at least not by the
rigid standards of 1972. She was a Japanese businessman as-
signed to a dreary job in a London office. But when she came to
us, she was beautiful. And I don't mean just in our sympathetic,
loving trannie eyes. I don't know what Reiko looked like as a man,
but as a woman she was tall, austere, and stunning, even by the
rigid standards of 1972.

One evening she left her drab businessman body at home
and stepped out as Reiko. I imagine her walking in Mayfair, or
on Bond Street, both graceful and nervous, her movements more
elated with every step. At a certain point she stopped before a
store window, maybe to look at a sapphire necklace, or something
as simple as a shawl. She was standing there when she heard
people talking in Japanese about a beautiful woman. They were
admiring the woman's dress, her hair, her bearing. Quietly, Reiko
glanced around to see who it was, and discovered that there was
no one else, that they were talking about her. What they said
thrilled her, except – they were speaking in her own language.
They were standing a few feet away from her, and talking about
her as if they could not imagine she would understand a word
they were saying. Suddenly she realized. *They did not know she
was Japanese.*

She was tall, taller than most Japanese men, and in her high
heels impossibly tall for a Japanese woman. Or maybe they saw
she was trans, and while they admired the style and performance
they could not imagine that a Japanese man, whether executive
or salaryman, would ever do such a thing. Standing before that

shop window, bathed in the thrill of her true self, Reiko had lost her nationality, her language. She'd become an exile from a people who could not comprehend the possibility of her existence.

A True Story of the Future

Callisto saw her first High Trannie when she was young enough that she'd just undergone her third round of nano-vaccination. Five or six, I would guess. She herself just shrugs her soft wide shoulders like pillars of air and says she doesn't remember her age. Oh, but she remembers every detail of that first glimpse of the Living World.

From Callisto's description it must have been Katrina Harp, one of the five original Ghost Healers who founded the Nano-chine Society. She remembers that the woman – man – creature – floated a little off the ground. Probably what she was seeing were the visible traces of the nano cloud that swirls all about a High T. Callisto had been out walking with her mother, who may or may not have suspected that her sweet boy was infected with the Germ of Becoming, as someone once called whatever it is that makes us trans. If Mom did know, she probably suppressed the thought – even now, mothers still want to believe their children are normal – but she must have worried about something because she tried to keep little C. from looking. No chance. That five-year-old probably would have wrestled Mom to the ground if it were the only way to view that wondrous sight.

Harp, if that in fact is who she saw, was very tall, with gentle breasts and hips softened by a sheen of water that flowed up and down her body. Her long hair moved constantly, changing not just colour but form, sometimes a stream of bright particles, sometimes waves of light. She was wearing a ragged dress of many colours, probably nano-silk, while up and down the arms long wavering strands of light emerged directly from her nearly black skin. And there was writing on her. Words and symbols in unknown alphabets, diagrams, and drawings, they were written directly on her skin in yellow, blue, and lavender. She looked, Callisto said, like a treasure map to another universe. Which, of course, is what she was.

Harp bent down to face her. She was so tall, Callisto said, her knees looked like mountains, her face like the sun rising between them. "Don't be afraid," Harp said. "You and me, we dream the world."

"No," Callisto's mother said, but without much conviction. But when Harp opened her mouth to breathe on the child, and Mom saw the famous perfumed cloud, she grabbed her darling boy-child and ran off down the street as fast as she could wobble with a five-year-old pressed to her chest and belly.

"Poor Mommy," Callisto said to me once, as she rolled herself tighter into my arms. "I was struggling so hard to get down, or just to see, I'm surprised we didn't both collapse in the street."

"She should have let you," I said. "She was only delaying what had to happen."

"But she didn't know that, did she? She was just trying to protect me."

"You? Or herself?"

She shrugged, and the way we fit together shivered sweetly through my body. "I don't know," she said. "Maybe in her mind they were the same."

Two days later, Callisto was missing. Her parents ran up and down the streets, her father convinced that "that creature" had kidnapped their child. It was laughable, really. If Harp had wanted the child, she could have just sent a government team to adopt her. But why? We don't recruit. If you're not born a T. cell in the body of God, no nano sex change will make a difference. And it's not as if we're dying out. The fact is, many parents, either poor or just ambitious, dress their children in whatever they think looks trans in hopes they can propel the kid into the ranks of the people who rule their world. We send them home.

Callisto's parents finally found their baby at the edge of a river that ran past the housing complex a couple of miles from Callisto's home. Callisto had stolen one of her sister's dresses, a ruffly thing in white, and used the baby pocket knife Daddy had given her (she still has it, sometimes wears it on a gold chain around her neck) to slash it into tatters. She'd taken one of Mom's scarves as well, and cut streamers from it to tie on her arms and legs, and with a couple of crayons had written meaningless signs and pretend formulas in some imaginary language up and down her body.

She didn't hear her parents at first. She was staring at the water, imagining the river was her, imagining she was swept away, formless and bright, into an ocean of mystery at the end of the world.

Her mother screamed and ran up to grab her, though I'm sure she knew it was too late, it had always been too late. Callisto turned and spoke calmly, but not in any human language. "It was all squeaks and clicks," she said to me. "I didn't really have any idea what it was supposed to mean. I just thought it was what I'd seen written on her body."

Her mother started crying, but her father, a man of action, hit her across the face. Hearing this, I let my Old World instincts take over, and I assumed her father was "queerphobic," or whatever quaint term we used before genuine civilization came into the world. But no. He was a man of his time, after all. What he yelled was, "You think you're better than us? Gonna leave us behind and laugh at us? Gonna become one of *them*? You think creatures like that, with all their money and their nanomachine factories, you think they care about people like us?"

Callisto ran away five times growing up. It wasn't to escape her parents. After that first time they were more than a little afraid of her, and not very likely to harm her. And if they tried, she had learned from a trannie boy in school that she could report them to the Transgeneration Child Protection Agency. No, my little Callisto wasn't really running *away*. She was looking for people with writing on their bodies.

Over the years she found a few, including a lover, Hermes Tree, whose penis was so cleverly inscribed it displayed Orphic love poetry when collapsed, but when it opened up those same markings became part of detailed alchemical diagrams, what Hermes Tree called "the nano codes of creation." But she never found Harp again. Truth is, no one has seen Harp for thirty years. People claim to have sensed her, to feel her all around them, but her body seems to have freed itself from a fixed reality altogether.

When Callisto first transformed, she spent the entire seclusion time after the insertion talking to her nannies in that same made-up language in which she'd answered her mother years before. She'd decided not to write it out on the surface. It was only for her and "the children," as she called the microscopic tribe that created her and still lives inside her. But sometimes, when we make love, I can see the messages come awake under her skin, I can hear the nannies in her blood whistling and clicking to each other.

Sometimes afterwards, as our dissolved bodies come back together, Callisto will ask me for a story. "Tell me of the Old World," she said to me once. "Tell me how it changed, what it felt like."

"Okay," I said, "but I won't do it directly. Let me make a fairy tale out of it."

"Ah," she said, and smiled up at me with a face shining bright as the Sun.

The Beatrix Gates

Once upon a time, there was a girl named Kara, who lived in the Tribe of Red. Red people only ate food of that colour, just as the Tribe of Green only ate green food. People were just made that way. Their bodies were different, their skins varied shades of their tribe, their inner organs even formed differently. The good thing was that the Reds desired exactly their own kind of food and the Greens desired theirs. They lived in different parts of town, with Green or Red restaurants and shops, and everyone was happy.

Except for Kara. From as early as she could remember, she wanted to eat green food. And more, she wanted to wear green styled clothes, which were not all green, but shared certain styles and shapes and fabrics, and were cut to fit green bodies. Sometimes she worried that she wanted to leave her tribe altogether and become a Green. But that was impossible. God clearly had made her Red, and that was who she was. Yet − sometimes − if she was really honest with herself, if she felt deep inside to what was true, she didn't just *want* to be a Green, she believed, insanely, that she actually was.

It made no sense. She was not stupid or crazy, she could see herself in the mirror, a normal Red. Greens had a ridge over the eyebrows, lines on the sides of the neck, long fingers, a separated upper lip. Kara had none of that. She hated her flat forehead, her stubby fingers, but she knew they were there. But if she closed her eyes, stood in the centre of her bedroom, and said, "I am Kara, of the Tribe of Green," then her body opened up, and all her cells smiled. If she tried to take herself firmly in hand and say, "Don't be ridiculous. You know you're Red, you just need to grow up and accept it," her skin tightened, her cells shrank in on themselves, and her lungs wept and refused to take in any more air.

As a teenager, the desire for everything Green, but especially Green food, became overwhelming. When she couldn't stand it, she would go behind a Green restaurant or grocery and look for scraps of thrown away food that she ate so fast she came close to choking. This was dangerous, for if someone discovered her she would be arrested and ridiculed, maybe even beaten or put in a mental hospital. And even though it felt so good while she did it, afterwards she would lie in bed, hugging her shame and silently crying with the light off, lest her mother come ask what was wrong. Her mother loved her, and wanted the best for her, but the best would mean some kind of treatment to make her normal. How her father would react, she didn't want to think about.

Much more satisfying were the rare moments she could disguise herself as a Green and go out in the world, maybe even buy a meal in a Green fast food restaurant, one without a long line where people might have time to examine her closely. It wasn't easy. She needed to buy – or steal – Green clothing, along with devices and makeup to change the shape of her body. Even more difficult was finding a place to put it all on. Greens and Reds did mix in certain places, such as theatres or large department stores, but it was very dangerous to walk into a ladies' room as a Red and emerge as a Green. If she were caught, they'd lock her up as a dangerous pervert.

Could she really eat green food, or was she just fooling herself? It didn't make her throw up as every Red had always said it would (a girl at school had said, "If I even think of green food I get nauseous," and everyone agreed, even Kara, so no one would suspect her). But her body couldn't really digest it. When she was a child, she would pray every night to the Red God to let her go, and the Green God to change her so she could eat her "real" food, as she thought of it. Every morning, when she woke up and examined herself and discovered she was still Red, with Red clothes in the closet, and a Red mother who set out a bowl of berries for her, and a Red father who crunched red cereal in his thick red teeth, she prayed silently, "If you won't change me, kill me. Please kill me." As she got older, she stopped the prayers, but not the desire to die.

One day a new teacher, a Red of course, came to teach science at Kara's high school. He looked like everyone else, but there was an air about him, a kind of secret delight. Kara had to control herself from staring and staring. Finally, she deliberately messed up an exam so she could request a meeting to discuss her grade.

As soon as she was alone in the classroom with him she closed the door, strode up to him at his desk, and said, "You did it. You changed."

He got up to walk past her and open the door. "I have no idea what you're talking about."

She closed the door again. "You crossed over."

"Stop that," he said, and once more opened the door. "You want me to lose my job?"

"I'm sorry," she said, and then softly, "but I have to know how you did it. You were a Green and now you're a Red. *Please.*"

He tried to summon up a denial, to mold his face into *what-are-you-crazy*, but it fell apart in a burst of compassion. Instead he just looked at her, and with a sigh he walked over and shut the door.

He knew what she wanted, he told her. He'd known from the first day he'd seen her, and dreaded this moment, for it was a hard life, and even though it had its own beauty, no one could understand it. The best you could hope for was that you changed and no one would ever know. Worst of all, he said, was that it really wasn't anything you could choose. The desire, the need, was so strong it was like … he frowned.

Kara said, "Like being whipped by God."

His eyes widened, and then he smiled. "Yes."

"How?" she demanded. "How did you do it?"

He told her of a group of alchemical doctors hidden in a far desert, people who'd studied the essence of Green and Red, and ways to change bodies through herbs, scalpels, and even spirits so subtle they could enter the body through small cuts on the hands or merely through breathing. To find these people, she would have to travel through many lands and across dangerous territory. There was one thing that would help her. In every place, there were people like them. Some, like the teacher himself, had made the journey and returned, others were weak, either physically or emotionally, but they loved the ones who could do it, and helped them in any way they could. That way they might imagine they themselves were passing through the "Alchemist's Palace," finally able to eat the food they had craved all their lives. Together, all these people formed what they called the Underground Caravan to help the Changers on their way.

Kara didn't dare tell her parents what she was going to do. They would try to stop her, and if she got away, and succeeded, she would come back a Green, unable to live in their world of Redness ever again. She left them a letter to ask their forgiveness, saying only that she had to do the most important thing in her life and they would never see her again. With what little money she had, and the address of the nearest stop on the Underground Caravan, that tunnel through the world, she set out.

She travelled for two years, the hardest but also the most exciting time of her life. Even if she could have gone there directly it was very far away, but the path of help zigzagged so much she felt like a ball of dust blown from one corner of a room to another. When she ran out of money, she discovered there were men who would pay her to wear green clothes and eat green food until she vomited on herself. She hated them and sometimes imagined killing them even as she smiled and made loud smacking noises with her lips as she took a bite.

Finally she saw it. Kara had expected something grand and

ancient, with stone turrets or golden domes. Instead, she came over a hill of cracked brown dirt, with a green scarf wound around her face to protect her from what she thought of as red winds, and saw a low building of stone and glass. It looked like it had grown out of the desert floor. Over the stone, green and red vines twined together. Looking at them, Kara felt both queasy and excited.

Before she approached the building, she reached into her bag for a green cloak. She'd stolen it years ago from an unlocked house and kept it hidden under a pile of old toys in her parents' garage. Now she'd carried it on her journey and sometimes wrapped it around her when she slept, if she thought no one would spot her. She swirled it around her and fastened the clasp.

Kara didn't know what she expected. Maybe a kindly doctor would step out, or a group of Changed Greens who would welcome her with a platter of delicacies. Instead, a door opened and a tiger and leopard slinked out, each step slow and deliberate, as if they wanted to make clear there was no need to rush. The black eyes fixed on her, the teeth gave off sparks in the sun. Instead of yellow and black, the tiger was red with green stripes, the leopard green with blood-red spots.

Kara backed away. She looked all around, as if someone might rush up and rescue her, but there was no one. "Please," she said, not sure if she talked to the beasts or to someone hidden in the building. "It's not fair. I've come all the way across the world. I gave up everything."

"Not everything," the tiger said, and moved low to the ground, tensed to jump.

The cloak, she thought. They were punishing her for wearing a green cloak when she was still a Red. It was so unfair, they were supposed to be different, to help. Backing away, she reached up to the clasp. If she took it off, would they let her go? Maybe she could throw it at their heads so they couldn't see as she ran back over the hill.

No, she thought, with the clasp half-open. She'd rather die for real than run back to a dead life. She refastened the cloak and stepped forward. The tiger and leopard leapt at her throat.

Over the next weeks, Kara knew consciousness at only rare moments. There was pain, and stabs of pleasure, and tiny bursts of light that went off under her skin. Ghosts moved alongside her, Green and Red nurses and doctors. Sometimes she saw an old woman with loose silver hair, a long white dress, and skin so smooth and colourless it seemed almost transparent. Kara had never seen someone who was neither Red nor Green, and she would have stared if she'd not been too tired to keep her eyes open. The woman said her name was Beatrix. When she stroked Kara's forehead with the tips of her fingers, green light ran through Kara's body.

Kara woke up for real in a green wooden bed, under a green cover. She realized she was wearing a green nightdress, while alongside the bed a green robe lay over a wooden chair painted all over with green vines. Ignoring the wobbliness in her legs, Kara jumped up and ran to a mirror on the side wall. Yes! She could see the change in her face and skin. She was Green! And hungry, un-equivocally hungry, with no more horrible choice of eating food she hated or food her body could not really accept.

Just then a man came in, a young Red with a silver tray of food, all of it green, green, green. He laughed happily at her greedy appetite, her sighs of delight. It sounded like the laughter of someone who knew just how it felt. It struck Kara – she'd nev-er thought this before – that as much as she was Green, and had always been Green, she was something else as well. She belonged to a secret tribe, the Changers. Her bond with this transformed Red, this man she didn't know and could never be close to in the outside world, might be stronger than with any Green she would ever meet. She thought of all the Greens and Reds who'd helped her find her way to the Alchemist's Palace. She reached over to hug the young nurse. What would outsiders think of *that*? A Green hugging a Red. They both laughed.

She sat down on the chair. "Is Beatrix here?"

Nurse Red stared at her. "Beatrix?" he said softly. "You saw her?"

"Yes, of course," Kara said. "She helped me when I was hurting."

"Just a moment." He got up and left the room. A few minutes later he came back with a short elderly man, a dark-skinned Green in an elegant white suit. "Good morning," he said. "I am Dr Virgilian."

"Oh," she said. "Were you the one – did you change me?"

"Yes. Many of us worked on you, but I led them."

"Thank you! Thank you so much!"

"Rosso tells me you were visited by a woman named Beatrix. Would you mind telling me what she looked like?"

"Of course," Kara said. She described the old woman, and added, "I assumed she worked here."

"Not exactly," Dr Virgilian said. "She shows up from time to time. On a volunteer basis."

"Oh. Well, if you see her, could you tell her I want to thank her? She was really very nice to me."

"Yes, certainly. Tell me something, Kara. Are you happy? Now that you've changed."

"Oh yes. This is all I've ever wanted. Thank you so much."

Dr Virgilian smiled. "Then we are happy as well. Congratulations, Kara. Welcome to your new life." He clasped both her hands in his for a moment, then bowed slightly before he walked to the door. With his hand on the knob he turned and said, "Feel free to explore the building and the grounds. And if I don't see you again before you return to the world please remember that you are always welcome here."

"Thank you," she said.

"Oh, by the way," he added, "the name Beatrix? It means 'she who brings happiness.' I looked it up once. Isn't that interesting?"

Kara stayed for over a week. She watched the Alchemists in their laboratories, whose walls were covered with symbols and formulas. She talked with other "transcolourists," a term she learned from Rosso, who himself had come years ago expecting to change and leave, but had decided there was no place he would rather be.

One afternoon she was sitting in a sun room with a young man named Willem, a New Green like Kara herself. Kara asked, "Were you scared out of your mind when that tiger and leopard came out?"

Willem squinted at her. "What?"

Kara wanted to run from the room. She said, "You know, when you first came to the Palace."

"I don't know what you mean. I knocked on the door and Rosso opened it and welcomed me. I was very happy I did not have to explain anything."

"Oh," Kara said. She felt herself shiver, and hugged herself. "I've got to go." All that day she wanted to ask Rosso or even Dr Virgilian, but didn't want them to think she was crazy. She must have passed out from hunger and dreamed it all.

The night before she was due to return to the world, Green Kara woke up to a strange sound. A mix of sustained high-pitched notes and low, sharply punctuated cries, it seemed a kind of singing, but nothing she'd ever heard or imagined. She was not even sure if it was human.

She put on her green robe and stepped into the empty corridor. Where was everybody? Couldn't they hear it? She walked towards the sounds. After various turns down different passages, she came to a spiral staircase she'd never seen before. She squinted up at it, confused, for it seemed to be taller than the building itself. It was dark, but at the very top she could see points of colour, and a shimmering line of white. Beatrix?

Kara climbed the spiral staircase for a long time. With every turn, the singing (if that was what it was) became louder, the high notes piercing her skin, the low a shock to her bones. A couple of times she tripped and almost rolled down again, but managed to stop herself so she could push upwards.

The first thing she saw when she reached the top was the open gate. There were two doors, one green, the other red, both engraved with complex diagrams that looked like messages. On the other side of the opening, she saw first nothing but darkness and tiny lights that appeared and disappeared, with swirling lines that seemed to vanish in on themselves. As she continued to stare, she thought she saw the tiger and leopard, fighting or dancing with each other, so fast she could hardly see them. And there were people, or at least she thought there were, so difficult to see. Maybe it was just a trick of the lights, for now she could see colour and pattern, green and red, and colours that Kara's eyes couldn't even figure out. She stared, her mouth open, her fists clenched.

It took a few moments before she saw Beatrix on the left side of the gates. Her white dress shone dimly in the dark. She said, "Beloved Kara. The Gates are open for you. You may enter or leave. There is no blame."

Kara lifted a foot. If she passed through, she would become something she couldn't even imagine. She would know rushes of colour and tone most people never suspected. Except – she would have to give up her life as a Green. There were no Greens or Reds beyond the gates, only colour that never ended and never stayed the same. "I'm sorry," she said to Beatrix. "I waited so long. I'm sorry." She turned and ran, as fast as she could, down to the solid ground of the Alchemist's Palace.

The trip back to the world was much easier than the journey out. Rosso gave her money and maps, and now that she was a proper Green she could eat and be with her own people, whenever she wanted. She found a town she liked, and got a job, and went back to school, and eventually became a librarian. She made friends, even fell in love a couple of times, though never for very long. How could she tell a lover the most important thing about her? It was only late at night that she sometimes wondered, just what *was* that thing? That she had been a Red and was now a Green? Or that she passed up the chance to become something else?

She joined the transcolour underground network, sheltering travellers and directing them to the next stop. She helped so many, they called her "the Travel Agent." She found small groups of neo-greens, and even a mixed group of Greens and Reds. It thrilled her to discover how much their lives were like hers, the childhood of loneliness and fear, the desire that made you feel like a leaf in a hurricane of fire. And then the discovery of hope, the ecstasy of change. But she never mentioned the tiger and leopard, or the singing, or the doorway she thought of as the Beatrix Gates.

After fifteen years had gone by, Kara travelled back to her hometown. For a week she stayed in a Green hotel, went to all the Green restaurants, and the Green markets. She watched groups of teenaged Green girls, or Green children in their Green playground. Finally, she took a taxi to her parents' home and rang the bell.

Kara's mother answered the door. Her face sagged a little, and she looked shorter, but she was dressed more carefully than Kara remembered, in a red skirt and jacket that looked almost elegant. Distaste flickered in her face before she coated it with politeness. It was nothing personal, Kara knew, just what any Red feels towards a Green who shows up on her doorstep. Kara had felt the same way once, when a Red plumber came to fix her toilet.

"Can I help you?" Kara's mother said.

"Mom," Kara said, "it's me. Kara."

"What?"

"I've changed, Mom. I always wanted to change and I did it. That was why I left. But it's me. I missed you."

"How dare you?" her mother said. "I don't know who you think you are or who sent you with that sick joke."

"It's not a joke. I'm your daughter."

"My daughter was Red. Can't you see that? What's the matter with you? She was a beautiful Red girl and she disappeared a long time ago. Some Green pervert must have taken her. If you don't get out of here right now, I'm calling the police."

"Mom, please...." Kara's mother slammed the door. Kara walked away.

Years passed. Kara became head of the regional library system, where she promoted books on openness and tolerance. She continued her work with the Underground Caravan, and even received an award at a secret convention deep in the mountains. She hid the plaque – gold, with green and red swirls that reminded her of the Palace – in the bottom drawer of her night table.

One evening, at a Green health club, she met a school teacher named Devra, who was bright and funny. They went for a drink, and then the next night dinner, and soon they were lovers. Devra was wonderful and Kara even thought she loved her. But after some months, Devra wanted marriage, and while Kara thought this would be wonderful, and could even imagine them as old women together in a house by the sea, she knew she could not get married without telling Devra her secret. She broke it off. For some time she berated herself for cowardice, and a too-long habit of secrecy. Then one night, as she was sitting alone with a glass of green Curaçao, it struck her that she wouldn't know what to say. In the years before she'd changed, she would have known exactly what to say, the same narrative she now heard over and over from the people she helped. Something shifted, however, that last night in the Palace. It left her with a riddle that seemed beyond solution.

As time went on, a new spirit of openness stirred in Kara's country. People talked about Greens and Reds becoming friends, even lovers, though many wondered how this could happen since sharing food was so important in romance, and they'd get sick if they even cooked together.

One Sunday morning, Kara sat down with a cup of green tea and the paper. Suddenly she gave a cry and spilled her tea. The magazine cover showed a handsome adolescent Green staring out at the camera. The lighting allowed his face to shine while hiding his clothes. You could see the eyebrow ridge, the separated lip, the lines in the neck that clearly marked him a Green. Across the bottom of the page, in bright pink, were the words "I Am A Red!"

Kara read the article three times and might have read it forever if the phone calls hadn't started. Everything was there: the longing, the hopelessness, the constant thoughts of suicide. There were various attempts at explanations, talk of nature's (or God's) mistakes, fetal brain chemistry, and so on, none of which interested Kara in the slightest. More important was the claim that the "condition," while very rare, occurred in Greens and Reds of every culture.

Would people suspect her? Kara wondered. Her best guess was no, though her hands shook even as she pretended to think calmly. She'd been Green for so long, was so established, looked just any other middle-aged Green woman.

Some of the callers worried about their own safety. Others hoped the outside world would become more tolerant. Still others worried if the Caravan would have to increase security, and what it all might mean to the Alchemist's Palace. After several hours, Kara stopped answering the phone.

She went and lay down on her bed, stared up at the pale green ceiling. What did it all mean? If it all became public, maybe even accepted, would that make it normal? Or understood? Did she herself understand anything?

To Kara's relief, no great change happened. People discussed the article with fascination or disgust. Some made jokes about it, or claimed it was all a hoax. Kara took a tolerant stand admired by many of her friends. Soon the question was mostly forgotten.

One day, thirty-two years after she'd left the red and green building in the desert, Kara saw a sign outside a planetarium. "Music of the Spheres," it read. "Ancient dream, modern reality?" She was in a city new to her, for a conference, and had the afternoon free, so she stepped inside.

The planetarium was a circular room with a dome-like ceiling and wide seats that tilted back like dentist's chairs. Though there was no official separation, custom gave the left side to Greens, the right to Reds. Kara sat down among a class of chattering high school students. There was more space on the right, but you just didn't do that. She would have been uncomfortable, even if no one else were sitting there.

The room went dark and the ceiling lit up with an old-fashioned image of the heavens, a blue-black sky with the constellations marked in dotted lines. A man's recorded voice intoned platitudes about the ancients' belief in gods and spirits. The image shifted to concentric circles with the earth in the centre and small circles labeled with the names of the sun, moon, and planets. The speaker told how people believed that the earth was at the centre of a series of spheres, each one with its own musical tone corresponding to the diatonic scale. Sonorous sounds echoed around the room.

Sadly, the voice said, this vision of harmony ended (*sudden silence*) when people discovered that the universe was vastly greater than the solar system, with the earth a speck at the edge of a mundane galaxy. Now the image shifted to swirls of colour, red and green, but also blue, yellow, purple, all rushing away and replaced by new explosions of light.

Has the music ended, the voice asked, and answered itself no. A different kind of music has emerged, more subtle and far stranger. A deep hum sounded – the background radiation of the Big Bang, the voice explained. Higher electronic notes followed, a supposed version of the radio waves given off by stars and faraway galaxies, followed by staccato sounds that represented pulsars. The universe sings to us all the time, the voice proclaimed. We are not equipped to hear it but we know it is there.

No, Kara thought. We can hear it. We have to open ourselves, not just our ears but our whole bodies. We have to become something … no longer human? No longer Red or Green, or any fixed colour at all. But the singing, the voices, the *invitation*, is always there. It never stops, ever.

She was shaking now. The teenage girl next to her edged away, whispered to her friend who looked over at Kara and giggled. Kara didn't care. She knew at last what she'd heard that night at the Palace. It was the universe itself, singing to her. The people she saw were the ones who had gone through, and they all sang to her through the deep longing in the curve of space, the passionate love that spiraled through galaxies. And they didn't just sing of the vast cosmos. Her own cells, the mighty civilizations of molecules and atoms that made up her body, the leptons and baryons and all the patterns between them, they were all held together by music, the songs of desire.

She had to leave. She stood up, ignored the grunts and whispers of the teenagers. With just the slightest shift, she could pass right through their bodies. Like her, all they were was music.

She rushed out of the building, stood among the trees outside the museum. She closed her eyes and realized she didn't know if the trees were red or green. She held her arms out slightly from her body, the hands opened, the fingers pointed at the ground. She realized it now. *She'd never stopped hearing it.* She could hear it right now, she'd been hearing it for thirty-two years. She'd only pretended to herself that it ended when she ran down the stairs. It never ended, she heard it in her fingers, in the breath of everyone around her, in the leaves, the trash in the street, the dirt, the electrons that surged through the concrete.

And something more. She was still there. Still at the top of the staircase, still staring through the Beatrix Gates. She'd never left.

Oh, she knew very well that her body, middle-aged and green, stood upright on a street, outside a building of steel and concrete and glass. This was real, and the cars were real, and the pigeons (she could hear the clumsy flap of their wings), the shoppers and commuters, the automatic doors that hissed open and closed. They were all real. But so were the Gates at the top of the stairs. In every moment, whatever she did – drinking green coffee at her desk, talking on the phone to another helper from the Caravan, making precious Green love to Devra (did that too go on forever and ever?), crying outside her mother's red door, half-asleep in her bathtub after a long workday, praying for death when she was nine years old – at every moment she *also* stood, shaking and frightened and newly Green, at the top of a spiral, before a woman who was old and young and colourless and every colour at once, and beyond her the forever open Gates.

Could she will herself there? Right now? Vanish from the street and reappear at the doorway? Eyes still closed, she drew her body into herself, arms across her chest, feet together, chin down. She tried to let the music fill her, expand her, make her a pulse of sound. No. The songs were real, and the

Gates, and Beatrix, serene and patient, but so were the buses and the museum building and the couple arguing down the street. She laughed and opened her eyes. All right then, she would do it the old-fashioned way.

She set off down the street towards the garage with her little green car in it, and with every step the universe surged alongside her. A block before the garage entrance she saw a Green boy, about seven, crouched down in a doorway. He was playing intensely with a two-inch-high action figure. "Captain Red," it was called. Kara'd seen it once on TV. Every few seconds the boy's eyes flicked up, then back to his toy. Heaven pulsed in his chest.

Kara bent down in front of him, watched him cringe and hide the toy in his pocket. She knew it was the most precious thing he'd ever owned. "It's all right," she told him. "You're a good boy." She wanted to say, "The sky loves you," but he wouldn't understand. Very carefully she said, "When I was your age, I was Red."

He stared at the ridge over her eyes, the rich green of her face and hands. "Yes," she said, "it's true. You can change. It can happen." Now she got out a pen and a scrap of paper from her purse and in green ink wrote down a phone number. "Hide this somewhere," she said as she gave it to him. "And memorize the number in case you can't keep it. When you're ready call them and say that Kara the Travel Agent wants them to guide you. Do you understand?" He nodded. Kara said, "You need to say it."

He whispered, "Yes."

Kara smiled and gently kissed the top of his head. Galaxies swirled under his scalp. "We have been here forever," she said.

Kara's second journey to the Alchemists' Palace took less than a quarter of the time of the first. She knew the way, and she had a car, and people to help her. She arrived on a chilly winter afternoon, with the faded old cloak – she'd saved it all these years – once more wrapped around her.

The tiger and the leopard were waiting outside the building before she arrived. She stood before them, arms out and welcoming. "I'm ready," she said. But instead of mauling her, they just rubbed her legs like kittens, then urged her around the corner to a yellow door she'd never seen before. When she opened the door, there it was: the spiral staircase.

All along the journey she had imagined herself running up the stairs, lifted by the music and her own joy. Now she moved very slowly, each step deliberate, for she wanted the entire experience. She first saw Beatrix about halfway up. The spiral turned her towards and away and she would twist her head to try to keep the woman in sight, as if she might vanish, and the singing stop, the moment Kara lost sight of her.

When she reached the Gates, they looked duller than she remembered. There were no flashes of light or sudden flares of colour, no mysterious figures waiting for her, and she panicked that she might have made a mistake. It was the music that sustained her. It thrilled her, vibrated her veins and stretched her skin, so that she thought she might break apart at any moment.

Then she realized why the Gates seemed dull, or empty. She was staring at colours she'd never known existed. There were tones and brightnesses for which she had no words, and so her mind had tried not to see them. She closed her eyes, opened them, and waves of colour swamped her. She could see people in them, and animals and landscapes, all of it shimmers of impossible colour.

At the top, she took Beatrix's hands, so thin and translucent. "I'm sorry," she said. "For staying away so long."

"I was always with you," Beatrix said.

"Are you coming now? Through the Gates?"

Beatrix shook her head, and for a moment the silver hair became all those colours beyond colour. Then it was once more ancient silver, as Beatrix said, "You are not the last."

Kara leaned forward and kissed Beatrix on the lips. Suddenly she discovered she was on the other side. *The Gates are my own body*, she thought. She was here, and Green, and Red, and every colour possible and not possible, surrounded by lovers and worlds as strange and wondrous as Kara herself.

She was every colour, and she was nothing, nothing at all. Nothing singing. Nothing filled with the music of everything.

Could she have gone to this place without all the struggle to change her colour? If Green and Red were so limited, couldn't she just have jumped past them? No. She knew the answer immediately. She had to become who she really was before she could become nothing. The key that opened the Beatrix Gates was passion.

And with that understanding, once upon a time ended, and she lived happily ever after, forever and never.

Something That Happened Long Ago
For two years in the last century before the world changed, I wrote a comic book. It was called *Doom Patrol*, and it told of a group of superheroes who all had terrible problems with their bodies. There was a head with no body at all, and a robot with a human brain, and a couple who were pure energy contained in bandages to give them a physical form, and a girl who was so ugly no one had ever loved her so that she created imaginary friends, each with its own super-power. Into this mix, I introduced Kate Godwin, a.k.a. Coagula, a transsexual lesbian superhero. Kate could dissolve and coagulate any form of matter (the result of sex with an alchemist), but her real super-power was much simpler. She accepted herself. She became the team's emotional leader, guiding them through various close calls with the end of the world (the book was prophetic) because she trusted desire.

After several months of Kate's stories, a letter came to us

from a reader in England. She called herself M.A. She wrote, "You have given me the courage to realize I do not have to feel ashamed of who I really am." And, "For as long as I can remember I have been miserable and only carried on living because I was too afraid that death would hurt too much. I did not realize that I was dead all the time. When I was a child I would pray to God every night that when I woke up in the morning I would have changed, of course I never did." And, "Thanks to the message you have conveyed using 'Kate,' and the support I have gotten from friends since I told them, I now feel that I can do something about my situation, that before I never really perceived I could alter."

Several years later, I went to a movie called *A.I.* in which a woman rejects her android son. Imprinted with love for his mother forever, the android remembers the story *Pinocchio*, in which a Blue Fairy changes a puppet to a real boy. The android boy thinks how if he became real then his mother would love him. He travels across the country until he finds a statue of a woman in a sunken amusement park. The woman is blue, and the android sits in front of it, underwater, for a thousand years, saying, over and over, "Please, Blue Fairy. Make me a real boy. Please, Blue Fairy. Make me a real boy. Please, Blue Fairy. Make me a real boy."

I sat in the movie theatre, and I watched the child, knowing it didn't matter whether it was boy or girl, the prayer was to become real. And I thought to myself, *The Blue Fairy couldn't do it. God couldn't do it. I did it.*

The magic formula to make someone real is very simple. Trust their desire. Believe in passion.

THIS IS A TRUE STORY. It is all a true story, and a very old one.

About the Contributors:

Diana Churchill lives in Newmarket, Ontario and began her career as a social worker after earning a Bachelor of Science and a Master of Social Work from the University of Toronto in 1988. In 1997, she launched her career as a freelance writer with a writing contract for a leadership education company and has since sold articles and writing services to websites, businesses, and educational consultants. Diana is a 2005 graduate of the Humber Creative Writing Program, in which she was privileged to work with Giller Prize-winner David Bergen on her unpublished novel, *All That She Desires*. "My Long Ago Sophia" is her first published short story, and is based on a character from that novel.

Candas Jane Dorsey is author of the novels *Black Wine* (winner of the James Tiptree Award, the Prix Aurora Award, and the Crawford Fantasy Award) and *A Paradigm of Earth*. In 1986, she won the International Three-Day Novel Contest for *Hardwired Angel*, written in collaboration with Nora Abercrombie. Her short fiction has been collected in *Machine Sex and Other Stories* and *Vanilla and Other Stories*. She has edited numerous anthologies, including *Prairie Fire: Canadian Speculative Fiction*, and two volumes in the *Tesseracts* anthology series. She won an Aurora Award for her short story "Sleeping in a Box," and her short fiction is included in many anthologies, including *The Norton Book of Science Fiction* and *The Penguin Book of Modern Fantasy by Women*, among others. She lives in Edmonton, Alberta.

L. Timmel Duchamp is the author of *Love's Body, Dancing in Time*, a collection of short fiction; *The Grand Conversation: Essays*; the short novel *The Red Rose Rages (Bleeding)*, and *Alanya to Alanya* and *Renegade*, the first two novels of the Marq'ssan Cycle. She is also the editor of an anthology of epistolary fantasies, *Talking Back*. Her stories have appeared in a variety of venues, including *Asimov's SF* and the *Full Spectrum, Leviathan*, and the *Bending the Landscape* anthology series, and she has been a finalist for the Nebula and Sturgeon awards and shortlisted several times for the Tiptree Award. She has also published numerous critical essays in *The New York Review of Science Fiction, Extrapolation, Foundation*, and *Lady Churchill's Rosebud Wristlet*,

a selection of which can be found on her website: *ltimmel.home.
mindspring.com.*

Neil Gaiman is a polymath, working in almost all forms of media,
including fiction, poetry, song lyrics, film, and graphic novels. A prolific
author of comics, his best known work in the field is the comic series *The
Sandman*, which he wrote for seventy-five issues, which are collected
in ten volumes. Other comic work includes *Violent Cases, Signal to
Noise, Black Orchid,* and *The Books of Magic*. With Terry Pratchett, he
is author of the novel *Good Omens*. His solo novels include *American
Gods, Anansi Boys, Stardust,* and *Coraline*. He is author of two children's
picture books, illustrated by Dave McKean: *The Day I Swapped my
Dad for Two Goldfish* and *The Wolves in the Walls*. He wrote the BBC
miniseries *Neverwhere*, later published as a novel as well. His most
recent film is *Mirrormask*, created with long-time collaborator Dave
McKean. He has won thirteen Eisner Awards, three Nebula Awards,
three Hugo Awards, three World Horror Awards, the World Fantasy
Award, and the Mythopoeic Award. His website, featuring his popular
blog, is *neilgaiman.com.*

Hiromi Goto's third novel, *The Kappa Child*, won the James Tiptree,
Jr Award and was nominated for the Sunburst Award. Goto was born in
Chiba-ken, Japan, and immigrated to Canada with her family in 1969,
eventually arriving in Alberta. Her first novel, *Chorus of Mushrooms*,
examined the immigration experience of Japanese Canadians through
the lives of three generations of women in a Japanese family living in a
small prairie town; it was the 1995 regional winner of the Commonwealth
Writers' Prize for Best First Book, and co-winner of the Japan-Canada
Book Award. Her second book was a young adult novel, *The Water of
Possibility*. She is also author of a collection of short stories, *Hopeful
Monsters*, published by Arsenal Pulp Press. Goto now lives in British
Columbia and has a new YA novel, *Half World*, forthcoming from
Penguin.

Joy Parks sometimes finds herself nostalgic for a past she never lived. In
her perfect world, there would still be dress-up cocktail parties, summer
kitchens, five-cent banana popsicles, and a future that keeps us on the
edge of our seats. After writing for years about GLBT literature for
both mainstream and community media, she began writing fiction as a

fortieth birthday present to herself and has since published stories in several anthologies.

Rachel Pollack is the author of twenty-nine books, including *Godmother Night*, winner of the World Fantasy Award, and *Unquenchable Fire*, winner of the Arthur C. Clarke Award. Her most recent work is *The See of Logos*, a set of surreal fortune-telling cards. A renowned Tarot expert, she is author of *Seventy-Eight Degrees of Wisdom*, often described as the "bible" of modern tarot interpretation, and has created various tarot decks, including the Shining Woman tarot. She has also written scripts for numerous comics, most-notably *Doom Patrol*, where she introduced the first transexual lesbian superhero in comics. In 1993, she addressed a meeting of the forty-nation Council of Europe on the subject of "Transsexualism and the Law." Her website is *rachelpollack. com*.

Caro Soles is a Canadian author of mysteries and SF, including *The Abulon Dance, The Tangled Boy,* and the forthcoming *Drag Queen in the Court of Death*. Under the pseudonym Kyle Stone, she is author of numerous books of gay male erotica, including *The Citadel, The Initiation of P.B. 500, Fire & Ice, The Hidden Slave, Rituals,* and *Fantasy Board*. She is the founder of Bloody Words, Canada's biggest annual mystery writing gathering. Her website is *carosoles.com*.

Bryan Talbot is a British comic artist and writer, best known for his ambitious comics series *The Adventures of Luther Arkwright* and its sequel *Heart of Empire*. His graphic novel, *The Tale of One Bad Rat*, won an Eisner Award, a Comic Creators' Guild award, two UK Comic Art awards, two US Comic Buyers' Guide Don Thomson awards, and the Internet Comic award for Best Graphic Novel. He has also worked on comics with other creators, *Hellblazer, The Sandman,* and *Batman*. His official fansite is *bryan-talbot.com*.

About the Editors:

Richard Labonté lives some of the time in a wee Perth, Ontario apartment, and some of the time in a ten-bedroom farmhouse on 200 acres of land near Calabogie, Ontario. From 1979 to 2000, he helped found and then managed A Different Light Bookstores in Los Angeles, West Hollywood, and San Francisco. He has edited the *Best Gay Erotica* series for Cleis Press since 1997; reviews 100 books a year for Q Syndicate, which distributes his fortnightly column "Book Marks" to a number of gay papers and websites; writes the subscription newsletter "Books to Watch Out For/Gay Men's Edition"; writes book reviews for *Publishers Weekly*; and, to make a living, edits technical writing. His husband Asa, who he met in San Francisco in 1992 and married in Ontario in 2003, is waiting patiently for his application for Canadian permanent residency to be processed.

Lawrence Schimel is an author and anthologist, who has published over seventy books, including *Two Boys in Love, The Drag Queen of Elfland, Kosher Meat, Things Invisible to See: Lesbian and Gay Tales of Magic Realism, Two Hearts Desire: Gay Couples on their Love, The Mammoth Book of Gay Erotica,* and *Vacation in Ibiza*. His *PoMoSexuals: Challenging Assumptions About Gender and Sexuality* (edited with Carol Queen) won a Lambda Literary Award in 1998, and he has also been a Lambda Award finalist ten other times. The German edition of his anthology *Switch Hitters: Lesbians Write Gay Male Erotica and Gay Men Write Lesbian Erotica* (also with Carol Queen) won the Siegesseuele Best Book of the Year Award. He won the Rhysling Award for Poetry in 2002 and his children's book *No hay nada como el original* (illustrated by Sara Rojo Pérez) was selected by the International Youth Library in Munich for the White Ravens 2005. His work has been anthologized in *The Random House Book of Science Fiction Stories, The Best of Best Gay Erotica, The Mammoth Book of Gay Short Stories, Chicken Soup for the Horse-Lover's Soul 2,* and *The Random House Treasury of Light Verse*, among many others, and has been translated into twenty-one other languages. For two years, he served as co-chair of the Publishing Triangle, an organization of lesbians and gay men in the publishing industry. Born in New York City in 1971, he lives in Madrid, Spain.